My Lady Glamis

Other books by Pamela Hill:

Tsar's Woman
The House of Cray
A Place of Ravens
Fire Opal
Daneclere
Stranger's Forest
The Green Salamander
Norah
Whitton's Folly
The Heatherton Heritage
The Malvie Inheritance
The Devil of Aske

My Lady
Glamis

Pamela Hill

St. Martin's Press
New York

Library of Congress Cataloging in Publication Data

Hill, Pamela.
  My Lady Glamis.

    1. Scotland—History—James V, 1513–1542—Fiction.
I. Title.
PR6058.I446M9   1987   823'.914   86-24783
ISBN 0-312-00162-2

First published in Great Britain by Robert Hale Limited.

First U.S. Edition

10 9 8 7 6 5 4 3 2 1

With sincere admiration for
another lady of Glamis

1

It was a summer's day when the Earl of Angus, not yet twenty, rode out with his young sister Jonet through the fair Lothian country towards the west, leaving the grey choppy sea and the rose-red bulk of Tantallon rearing above it. Such men as remained were idle, there being no longer fear of war. Two men-at-arms rode, however, behind them now for safety, for one never knew at any time what might befall anyone unattended. But the men did not keep close, and the jingling sound of their harness and mail hardly intruded on the young pair's thoughts as they went.

Brother and sister rode well and gracefully, their spirited mounts setting off their good looks and fine clothes, he in a short doublet and high narrow ruff of the new fashion, which flattered the cocky angle of his head beneath its small plumed hat. He was proud of his shapely legs, cased fittingly in silk from France beneath the high leather riding-boots; they had helped him in his fortunes.

Jonet was different. Still very young, she wore a hood of green and matching kirtle, while her long sweet hair flew out from beneath the hood with the speed of their going. Her eyes were the colour of water in a cool place; her mouth curved naturally in a little smile, as though she listened always. Her slender hands lay ready and easy on the reins; they were capable hands, but delicate. She was said to be the loveliest girl in Scotland.

As they rode she wondered why they rode alone and why George, her second brother, who was forever at Archie's elbow with some new thing, was not with them. They had left him quarrelling with his heiress wife, and Jonet was pleased that Archie—one must remember to call him

Angus now, since the death of their grandfather—had chosen her company instead. No doubt he had a purpose. She waited to find out what it was he needed to say, being not like their busy sister Alison, who would have asked outright. The bulk of Hailes reared at them across the flat land, and to avoid passing by there—there was bad blood over his bygone Hepburn marriage—Angus dismounted, looked about him, then lifted his sister courteously down from the saddle. They left the horses with the two men and strolled, Jonet guarding her skirts in one hand, to a little hollow where gorse was, and sat down on the turf, long and green with summer. She stared at Hailes Castle, thinking not of it or of the Hepburns there but of quite a different place, a little place on a light rise, Bonkle of the Border where she had been born and where they had all lived as children. It had been less grand than nowadays. She could remember playing with George and Alison and Elizabeth and flighty Margaret and the rest, and William before he became a priest, round and round and across the green grass where linen lay drying. And their mother had been still beautiful, not careworn as she looked nowadays since the death of their father at Flodden. And another thing she could remember there, from far back; a most lovesome woman, her mother's sister Margaret Drummond, the late King's sweetheart, lifting her up as a babe and kissing her with lips themselves much kissed. Jonet could remember nothing of Aunt Margaret's face, only the veil of her dark hair. They said she had died of poison, not long after.

"Ye are far away, Jonet. Come back here; I would talk with ye regarding great matters."

The light careless voice sounded like a boy's; but Angus was man enough, as he knew. He took a daisy by its stalk where they sat and fancifully began to pull the petals off, counting one by one the fates; love, hate, marriage, a bachelor. He was none, and smiled as the last petal pulled out with its proper reply. He turned to his sister, shapely lips set pleasantly.

"I am listening, my lord." She had spread her green skirts, and sat waiting. He looked at her seated there on the grass, restfully disposed, her hands in her lap. If only the Queen's Grace were so, instead of being a spoilt, loose-fleshed woman who had once been fair but who had borne the dead King six children! It crossed Angus' mind that of all that brood only two had lived, the present King and his brother. Angus allowed his handsome brow to pucker; it was important that he in his turn should have a living heir. His young Hepburn wife had died in childbed the eve of Flodden, and the bairn with her. He had not cared for her greatly and was glad now to be free to follow his ambition. They had talked him into it, no doubt, old grand-father Drummond and the Bishop, but he had been ready enough. He and the Queen together . . . power in Scotland . . . if she bore him a son it would be the gate to all things, and he with no man to say him nay.

That brought him to the thing he had to say himself. He was glad to tell Jonet and none other except George, who already knew. The lass was no gossip. "I have to tell ye," he began, "a thing which no other must know, for the time." It would come out in the end, of course; but Angus' mind pictured the future dimly as yet, to be shaped by himself.

"Ye may trust me." The colour in her cheeks had flushed to pale rose. She was still young enough to be flattered that he had chosen her to guard a secret. Men seldom trusted women, and one must always listen to them in any case. Jonet did not know where she had got this wisdom. She stared at the daisies in the grass, and said nothing, drew no amazed breaths, till he had finished his tale.

He bent over and whispered in her ear, so that even the men-at-arms would hear nothing. "I am to wed the Queen now she is free of childbed. Tell no one."

She promised again, while her long lashes, dark at their tips, dropped over the water-green eyes. It would anger him if she showed anxiety. But she had met the Queen once and had not liked her. It was true that as a widow Margaret Tudor was to be pitied, in especial as the late King had left her pregnant with a last child when he rode off to be killed at Flodden. The young Duke of Ross had been born by now and had lived, like the King his elder brother, and with him was safe from the English, for a great wall had been built by the folk of Edinburgh to hinder the English foe's coming north to follow up their victory. But they had not come. Yet the Queen was still an Englishwoman, the very sister of Henry VIII, who had been absent from the country leaving his wife to send the Earl of Surrey and his armies to fight on that dark day nearly two years since, when almost all the lords of Scotland had been killed with the King. And Surrey had taken the dead King's body south and folk said Henry VIII had given it no burial. Archie—Angus—was one of the few Scots nobles to have ridden home, and the common folk had suffered too.

A shudder took her. Great affairs were cruel. Would it not be better to stay out of them and live in peace?

Angus was restless, and after his great news had sprung to his feet, taking her up with him. "Let us walk," he demanded, and they strolled arm in arm through the turf, past the gorse, past young growing summer trees, beyond Hailes. Angus cast a half-resentful glance across at the grey pile. "It was ours once," he said, "as half Scotland was ours. The Douglas blood is older than the King's; we were gotten by the Mormaers in the time when Douglases ruled from one end to another of the Pictish kingdom, from Tay and the ocean west to Isla and again to Esk. We have married the daughters of kings and been great in council."

Jonet let him talk, but thought her own thoughts; and one of them was that their grandfather, old Bell-the-Cat, had been so great in council that he had hanged the late King's father's favourites over the bridge at Lauder. And a King of Scots had stabbed a Douglas to death, and had lived. Maybe such things had had to happen; but there was no need for oneself to grow heady as if with new wine. She was proud of being a Douglas, but would say little of it; one's actions spoke, not words.

"Now we must speak of yourself," said Angus importantly. He cast a glance over her flawless beauty and then looked away; it was like plucking the petals from the flower he had lately mauled. Yet she should please Lord Glamis, or any man.

He made himself smile. "Ye keep close counsel, Jonet," he said. "Another woman would have been at me to say what it is, and what must be; but ye are silent."

"I am listening," she said, as she had said before. At the same time she was aware of her constant love for him; handsome Archie, always cock-a-hoop, winning his way with everyone, displeasing some but not caring. Maybe displeasure would do him some hurt yet; but she prayed that the day might never come. So intent was she on this prayer that she brought her mind back to what he was saying, with added awareness that he had been talking for some time.

". . . and he is so quarrelsome, although always in a good cause, that folk call him Clang-Causey, for he makes the causeway ring," Angus said. "But of all women, ye will contrive, Jonet, and will hold the place for our name in the north, where I have land and titles as ye ken, and George forbye, at Pittendriech. Make friends of the local folk; there are many feuds, but ye will heal them. I will come and go as I may. Although it is a far ride I will bring news, and my heart. And George will be oftener up than I. Pittendriech is nigh to Elgin. It was a good marriage with Isobel, the heir."

"They have words often now. How old is my lord Glamis?" She felt no urge to be so soon married; the man himself sounded hard and noisy. But she would do as her brother bade her; any other course would never have entered her mind.

"Older than yourself, a little; the way a husband should be. I ken naught against John Lyon save his hot temper, which no doubt may be easy cooled in his bed."

He looked at her in a teasing manner, and she felt the blood creeping up to her face. Angus, who knew about women, had the advantage of her, who knew nothing as yet of men. But he was serious a moment after.

"Marry him with goodwill, Jonet," he said. "I would give this charge to nobody but yourself; our other sisters are foolish. Without your help there might in the end be war in the north, the way it was in the late King's time. He quelled it by going there himself, but our King now is too young, and there is nobody to replace him between the wild Highlanders and the east-coast folk."

"Well, I will do it," she said agreeably. She knew that the Highland clans need not concern her much; they were mostly at the other side of Scotland, among the lochs and wild glens. But she would do her best to make this quarrelsome young Lord Glamis a good wife, and to keep the peace for Angus. He had much ado with his spread lands, no one man could control them all.

She asked one thing. "Does George know of this?" she said. Within herself she was faintly jealous of Geroge's constant companionship with their eldest brother. George was rough and outspoken, and Jonet felt that she herself would have made wiser company. But that was folly; men were men, and would be together.

"George and I have no secrets from one another," Angus stated proudly. "He will be your neighbour, and is my loyal man."

Well, she must accept the way things were; she was only a woman. The thought of leaving her family, her home, for an unknown place in the north chilled her for instants. But folk were the same wherever they might be; she would make friends at Glamis.

At any rate, now she knew why Angus had asked her to ride out with him this day. She allowed the men-at-arms to help her into the saddle although she could have sprung to it on her foot. So they rode home.

In a house in Edinburgh, an old man of nearly eighty years of age, who would soon be dead, sat waiting for a summons. At any time now the serving-man of Bell-the-Cat's son Gavin Douglas, newly Bishop of Dunkeld, would come and tell him that all was ready for the Queen's marriage to his, John Drummond's, own grandson, the young aspiring Earl of Angus. There was a lad with hope for the future! One's own blood would not die out, and, as before, would mix with that of royalty. It was not that the Tudors were so great; but in this Queen's ancestry were the Plantagenets who had once ruled England. They alone were worthy to mix with the Drummonds.

The sun slanted into the room and picked out the colours of the carpet on the table. Lord Drummond stared at them and reminded himself of the painted ceilings at Stobhall, his old home before he had started building his new castle in Perthshire. Dull red, gold, blue, green, the colour of slate, they passed by, the figures from Holy Writ and the prophets. He thought of his wife, lately dead; she had borne him many children, and suffered much through them. So had he; but his ambition never rested. Why, in the Drummond line were two Queens of Scotland; that had been the reason that, long ago, my lords had been against the late King's marrying Margaret Drummond. It would have given the house too much pride. There had been a Drummond Queen Margaret in King Davie's time, and Queen Annabella in the time of Robert III. They had been beautiful women; all Drummond women were beautiful. But his own son, long ago, had been a rebel against the law, and King James IV had had the head struck from his shoulders. It had been a bad time, with one's enemies rejoicing.

Yet he was still proud, old John Drummond, and still had hope; this marriage today would give him power through his daughter's son Angus. The widowed Queen had blood less high than their own; she should be glad of the match to strengthen her. Drummond blood, Douglas blood . . . blood always, pouring from the scaffold in a dark river when his son David had been executed by the King's order long ago. He had more daughters left than sons, accordingly, but the line was safe.

He shifted a little in his chair and the memory of his wife .came to him, trailing aimlessly through the rooms as she had done in her old age. She had long lost her recollection and would ask for folk who were dead. "Where are my dochters, where are the bonny creatures? I wanted Sib to kaim my hair."

Sibylla. Eupham. Margaret. They had all died that other black day, in agony, but he had not seen them till the women had washed off the vomit and excrement. By then they were beautiful, still and calm. Had they been poisoned because of the English marriage, or had it been mushrooms, as some said?

Whichever way it was, the Englishwoman had come, and had married the King with great public rejoicings ten, twelve years ago. They had called her the English Rose. Maybe she was still like a rose, with its petals blown. The old man grinned to himself at the thought. Margaret Tudor would be glad of the young strength of Archibald Angus, his grandson. It had been providential that young Angus' wife had died before he came riding home from the battle almost alone; there were few young men left at Court. Her Grace had had an eye for Archie's fine white teeth and fine calves, and it had been an easy matter to see that they met often. Now she was like a bitch in heat.

Ambition. It had started maybe when he had let his other daughter Beatrix, who was wanton, become the

leman of the King's cousin Jamie Hamilton, who was
Arran nowadays. They all had their titles and their new
ways. Beatrix' children were bastards. But it had meant
the King's meeting Margaret Drummond day by day, and
so . . . And she had been bonny. Margaret had been the
bonniest of all, lovelier than Queen Annabella, or the
other bad Drummon Queen of David II who had stirred up
Europe with her affairs, to no purpose.

Women. He need no longer have aught to do with them.
If he had any matter to discuss he would send for his good
kinsman John of Innerpeffray, and they would talk, and
John would bring his sterling good sense to whatever it
was. Oneself could not always be alone. This time, he had
the Douglases on his side, proud Gavin, often a poet, now a
Bishop, though not of St Andrews which Her Grace had
tried to get for him. Between them they had made this
marriage and Gavin would perform it today, today. It was
better than writing his poetry.

The marriage. Elizabeth Drummond's son and the
Queen of Scots. If the dead King's Drummond love had
been Queen, there might have been no Flodden.

The old man's head dropped on his breast and he fell
asleep. It would be his last attempt at power. When the
Bishop's man called to say that everything was ready he
had to wake him. Then my lord went, leaning on his staff,
to see the man and woman made one.

The wedding had been secret, for fear of my lords in
council. It had taken place before a little altar in Her
Grace's closet, with neither bride nor groom very fine, but
dressed as usual. Now it was evening and Margaret Tudor,
Queen of Scots and, by today's vows, Countess of Angus,
lay waiting in bed, her bright hair carefully combed and

spread on the pillows. She stroked her hair, knowing it was beautiful; and her skin was good. She told herself this, persuading herself that Gavin Douglas's—the Bishop's— poem written to her years ago, calling her Venus in her chariot, was well founded. And she was the English Rose. Even through all the trouble and fighting there had been, and the sad strain of events leading up to Flodden, there had always been homage to her beauty, though she was an Englishwoman born and the old enemy of all Scots.

She moved her stoutening body in pleasure. Soon, again, there would be a man in her bed. She had missed such attentions since the death of her husband, the late King James IV. He had been good to her though somewhat unfaithful, and she had come to love him; in the last letter she had written to her brother Harry before the war she had said "Our husband is ever the longer the better to us, as knows God." She had been loyal. At no time had she attempted to cross or betray James's plans. In fact it was better for her to be ruled, to have decisions made for her. No doubt that was why she had, this very day, married again; the thought of a man's strong will, of his body, his expressed wishes, excited her. Yet it was daring, what she had done; she, the King of England's elder sister and heir, to marry for her liking a young Scots Earl, and tell none!

Soon now he would come. The plump hands with their narrow fingers caressed the sheets, then her hair again. The waiting plagued her. She had bidden goodnight as usual to her children, young James V and the tiny Duke of Ross. It was strange to have borne children that had lived. One dead birth after another, or hope of life for months only, that had been the tale of her children by the King. Now she was the mother of a monarch and as such, entitled to be treated with respect, with dignity. No doubt Angus realised the need to be respectful. He had always hitherto been so, kissing her hands often and saying most things with his eyes. She hoped he would come soon, yet half-feared his coming; why?

She cast about in her woman's mind regarding it, and came back again to James, to Flodden, to his many wounds and, lastly, a stab through his throat within a lance's length of the English commander. Surrey had been at her own wedding ten years before and Margaret had never liked him. He was Duke of Norfolk now.

Flodden. A dead, flat name, a place in Northumberland she had never before heard tell of even on her triumphal bridal journey to the north, to this cold austere land overlaid with gilding and flowing with wine for joy of her, the English Rose, the pledge of never more war between Scotland and England. Yet within ten years war had come. They said it was because of her, Margaret's, jewels from her dead mother, which Harry had always refused to send. God knew a war would not have been fought over jewels. It was Harry's fault, swollen as he was with conceit and rich with gold from their father's coffers. Harry had not known how to spend the money except on fine gilt armour and ships and pikes against the French, the King of Scot's allies It was the pikes that had won at Flodden, lopping off the wooden hafts of Scots spears. And all James' grand French cannon and his great ship, the *Michael*, everything of that kind was gone, and she was left here alone, or had been until today . . . tonight.

Angus came in then. He was wearing a lightly furred bedgown and on his face was a little smile of triumph at his own cleverness. He was telling himself what he had often done before, that this woman, who desired him more than he her, was no great thing except for her mother, Elizabeth of York. The Douglases were greater than the Tudors. Margaret's father had been a Welsh nobody who had set himself up as King of England after the Wars of the Roses. He had been grasping and had screwed money out of the English in fines and taxes. His son was still spending the money. Later one would think of all that again . . .

"Come into bed, my lord."

It was said with complacency, very near; she had got

him here at last, and he would do his duty by her. He would
have custody of the two princes, whatever any of my lords
said. How loose in her flesh the woman had grown since
her last childbed! In the moments left to him, he remembered his wild Border mistress Janet of Traquair; the
flying black hair, the taut thighs, the habit of dancing and
laughing her harsh laughter and refusing to wear stay-
bones in her dresses, and caring for none. This woman was
softer, fairer, suppliant; let the thing be done. He would
get her with child as he had got Traquair Janet. Janet would
make a fine scene when she knew the Queen was his wife.

He kissed the Queen's hand, then her mouth. He
climbed between the sheets with her. "My lord, my lord,"
she breathed, "none must know of this."

"There will come a time when they must know," he said
confidently.

Afterwards she felt bewildered, tousled, appalled. He had
been rough with her. She could still feel the grip of his
hands on her used, flaccid flesh, and her hair was no longer
spread in seemly fashion on the pillow.

Angus had left. Stumbling back to his own chamber, he
fell on his bed and tried to sleep. The night's work had been
distasteful to him, and he could not account for the rest-
lessness of his own mind. He had taken women before; it
should not be so great a matter. He sought in the darkness
for some comfort to guide him, and said a random prayer.
He tried to think of the Mother of God, and saw her, robed,
calm and quiet, with the smiling face of his sister Jonet, as
if it could give him back innocence, coolness, and peace. He
would ride down to Tantallon soon, and see her; and
clumsy John Lyon should come down from the north so
that the betrothal could be solemnised and any discussion
about the tocher smoothed out. Matters would take their
course as he, Angus, had planned them. Plans . . . his were
so wide and far-reaching that his brain could no longer
encompass their end. There was perhaps no end; as the

Queen's husband he would grow more and more powerful, making the name of Douglas greater even than it had been in the time of their grandfather Bell-the-Cat when he had ruled the King. He, Archibald Angus, would rule not only the King but all Scotland. He would outdo those whose names had never been forgotten at Tantallon. There was King Robert the Bruce's Black Douglas who had fought till he became a legend and, later, had borne Bruce's heart towards the Holy Land; there was that other Black Douglas who had fallen by the treacherous knife of James II after doing many things gallantly. There were the young Douglases of the Black Dinner at Edinburgh Castle, whom the King's guardians feared so much that they made away with them after bearing in a boar's head on a trencher. There were the Red Douglases of his own cadet branch, of his blood. He fell asleep at last, forgetting them.

John Lyon, sixth Lord Glamis, was already riding to the south. He told himself that he had other business besides seeing for himself this Douglas wench. It would have been unmanly to show eagerness in a matter which had been arranged chiefly to give him greater standing with his neighbours. Yet a Lyon stood as high as any, and if he misliked the girl he would not take her. It was true that he had, on his own account or because of family feuds, fallen out with Ogilvies, Huntlys, Forbeses, and lastly hot-tongued George Douglas of Pittendriech himself. Glamis reminded himself that it was other folks' fault, never his own. He had been in the right of it. The burden of asserting his right day after day had begun to weigh on him a little; it would be welcome enough to have a helpmeet to whom he could unburden himself, if she were not a fool. As it was, the present haughty pride of the Red Douglases offended him. This Jonet need never think she was more nobly born than he; why, he had royal blood! Let her take issue with him on that or any other matter, and he would beat her.

Women should be kept in their place.

He jerked his strong chin at the lands and the towns through which they passed, riding with a train full armoured and, himself, before the standard-bearer who carried the streaming banner of the great lion rampant azure, on its argent ground. It was a reminder of the nearness of the Lyon clan to the Kings of Scotland with their lion rampant gules on or. Had not his ancestor married the Princess Joan, daughter of Robert II, King Blearie? And had not that same man been Clerk of the Privy Seal and the strongest noble in Scotland, so that by the end his enemies caused his death? The wisest man in the kingdom he had been, the White Lyon;

> *So true he was that he was ne'er found false,*
> *Expert he was to write and dyte full fair,*

and that in a time when few men, even noblemen, could hold a quill. It was something to be descended from such a man.

A small voice whispered to him; if that is so, you need not make so much noise. John Glamis searched in a part of his mind that was seldom disturbed, and found a thing he dared not think of, hardly dared remember; the sight of his father's body carried in under a bloodied sheet, murdered by the Ogilvies while John was still a child. And, soon afterwards, George, his brilliant elder brother whom he worshipped as everything a man ought to be, learned, handsome, witty, adept with the sword and lance, had died of a fever. So he, John Lyon, had at last become Glamis and lonely with it, and nobody to whom he might take his troubles, because his flighty mother was taken up with her new marriage to Huntly and cared nothing for him. Nobody cared for him and they shrugged and called him Clang-Causey for the trouble and clamour he made. Other folk never seemed to have to make trouble, only himself.

If this Jonet Douglas proved a comely woman, he would be glad enough of her.

He saw her at last, smiling shyly across the great hall of Tantallon with the crowned heart carved and embroidered everywhere and the great red arches letting in the sound of the sea. She was the loveliest lass he had ever seen, but he was not used to women, except his mother. What was he to say to Jonet Douglas? God be thanked, she had not a busy tongue, and so far had said nothing. Angus himself, and the second brother George who had come south, filled the air with their loud words, but for once he, Glamis, could not answer. It would be greater fortune to have this lass in his bed and at his board than he had ever let himself imagine. Women as a rule had either gold, looks or high birth, there was always some flaw, yet he could find none in Jonet. He would think of her afterwards constantly, his mind filled with the thought of her till she could come to him as his wife.

"A cup of wine, my Lord Glamis," Angus said with his careless smile. Wine would make the young man less tongue-tied, no doubt, but he had not been surprised at the effect on her bridegroom of the budding beauty of Jonet. She was like a witch already, and never had to say a word; men ran to do her will. She would be a loyal ambassador for him in the north, where he had lands but no leisure to visit them, and George could not be up at Pittendriech all the time. He must arrange the binding contract as soon as might be. Meantime, the tocher settled, young Glamis must go back north. It was not yet time to welcome him into the family.

2

There was great scandal in Scotland when the news of the Queen's marriage to Angus leaked out: old Lord Drummond struck a herald on the chest to show him his manners. The false English creature, to let any man usurp the dead King's place in her bed! Every man, woman and child in the land still mourned James IV, their red-haired King with the haunted, beautiful eyes. The haunting was for his own father's murder, which my lords had done while he was a lad, thereafter forcing James to the crown; and folk said he wore a heavy chain about his waist all his life in penance. He had been a familiar figure riding the roads, alone or with his court; on justice-ayres, on pilgrimage, to see his sprightly mistress whom he shared with old Bell-the-Cat at Darnaway. This Red Douglas now had done more; he shared the dead King's wife. Old men cast about in their memories to the time their grand-fathers had spoken of, when another widowed Queen of Scots, Joan Beaufort, had wed the Black Knight of Lorne after her husband James I's murder. But that had been for protection in troublous times. This was no such thing; every Scot living had been loyal to the dead King's widow, and his son. Sadly, folk remembered still the marriage of the Thistle and the Rose; the streets had run with wine and there had been pageants and great rejoicing, and the King, who could leap from the ground into the saddle, had ridden the length of the town with his new bride on his saddle-bow, her famous hair flowing. Now, the Rose of England had lain down with the first young man to ask her.

The people, murmuring in their anger, converged on the Castle, taking the long slope grim and steadfast. Fists were waved and abuse shouted; in the end, a hush fell over the crowd, for the Queen had come out, in person. Most of them had never heard her speak, and she spoke now; and showed that she was a Tudor. The little King, red-haired like his father, she held by one hand; on her other arm was the baby Duke of Ross, and behind came Angus, fingers over his mouth. It seemed she was the better man of the two.

"What would ye? The King? He is safe here; see him. Ourselves? We are here also, as ye may judge. Every man and woman among ye has wife or husband; do ye deny the like to us? Ring down the portcullis! Go to your homes!"

The great iron gate clanged down; and its sound cowed the crowd and made them remember that they were, when all was said, ordinary folk. It was Margaret Tudor's finest moment. But the late King would not have shut himself off so from them, and they went home in dejection. There had been nothing accomplished by the march, after all; but at least they had seen the the little King strong and sturdy, with his red hair showing under his cap.

Angus was scarcely proud of himself for having let his wife take the lead then; but what else could he have done? Asserting himself, he told her that she must come to Tantallon with him for safety. "The Douglas men-at-arms will not betray me; they will guard us well," he said. So they rode, as if for a short journey save for Her Grace's gear, leaving George Douglas to have a care to the King and his brother that none might steal them away. Margaret wailed at parting with her children, but Angus had his men-at-arms by; she must needs go, and told herself it was for her pleasure. They rode beyond town and wall, making a clatter in the streets, and reached the east as the sun came up, silvering the rose-red towers and crowned heart banner floating in the day.

But the sea howled always below. After a night of it the Queen complained that she loathed the sound, and the east-wind draughts that blew through the arches past arras and fire. Bell-the-Cat's great sword hung in the hall and no lesser man could wield it; what was that to her? At Linlithgow, her pleasant sunny palace, she had taken comfort in climbing to a high place, a small secret place, and watching for the King to ride home. There were memories of him even here, for once he had dug a trench about Tantallon when Bell-the-Cat disobeyed him, then made it up at Christmas by sending the old Earl a black velvet gown. Angus related the tale with some pride; Margaret looked at him with a sidelong glance. "Maybe," she said. "The Red Douglas knew his place by the end." But the Douglas writ ran here.

The gulls wheeled always against the grey sky, screaming. It was a forbidding place. Her Grace was suffering already from morning sickness, which did not improve her temper. The only one who could soothe her, and take time to admire her collection of wired head-dresses and gowns, was my lord's sister, young Jonet Douglas. The Queen would have her much about; the child had gentle fingers.

One day Jonet sat with her sisters Elizabeth and Margaret in the solar, putting in a stitch here and there at a cloth all the Douglas ladies were working at, to lie by the end on the altar of the Lady Chapel in brother William's priory of Coldinghame. It had a curving pattern of a vine with grapes, and the Agnus Dei in silver and gold. Jonet traced the Lamb's curling coat with a finger, her face wearing its little constant smile. George's lady, who had been busied brewing with the servants, looked in to chide her young sisters-in-law. Being a Douglas born as well as by marriage, Isobel Douglas could say what she liked.

"There is work to be done," she told the girls. "Not many of us are fine ladies enough to sit at our ease before noon."

Elizabeth shrugged and Margaret said nothing. Jonet raised her dark-fringed eyes.

"I must keep my hands clean," she said, "for Her Grace will send for me presently." Against Isobel's harsh voice hers was soft; George and his lady quarrelled always and it had maybe given Isobel a roughness of the throat. Be damned to Her Grace, the woman was thinking now; she wants this and wants that, and a tester to be raised above her at meals.

"She does not send for me," said Elizabeth.

Isobel tossed her head. "There are some new come to Tantallon that carry themselves as if they owned Scotland." She closed her mouth with a snap, and ostentatiously began seeing the maids wax the furniture; Margaret had to move from where she sat.

"Isobel, she is an anointed queen," Jonet said. She had faith in all such things; the Host, the consecrated figures in the church, blessing, anointing. Isobel laughed.

"Tell that to our brother next time he lays her on her back. And to be anointed is not to make a saint, God knows. She must learn to thole other folk."

"So must you," said Elizabeth.

Jonet stroked the embroidered satin with her white fingers and did not reply. It was useless to be at issue with Isobel. She remembered the dark, stocky young man they had brought to her not long ago, who had ridden down from the north and was said to be so quarrelsome. Would she and Clang-Causey have matters out night and day like Isobel and George together? If so there would be no peace. She must learn to hold her tongue, and this moment was as good as any other.

Elizabeth went out, followed by Margaret, who could stay at nothing long. Just then the woman who attended the Queen came down, disgruntled. She dropped a curtsy to Isobel and Jonet, and spoke to the last.

"Nothing will please her but that ye shall go and kaim her hair, my young lady. I have broken a tooth of the kaim; another will maybe fare better." She was a Douglas likewise, a bastard of old Bell-the-Cat like many servants at the castle.

Jonet rose, gathered her skirts and ascended the red stone stairs to Her Grace's chamber. Her expression was thoughtful; Angus and his royal wife fell out often nowadays, not only with high words like George and Isobel but with silences. She must try to mend it, if anyone might. All she needs, the girl thought, is someone to give her pleasure, admire some matter of hers. It was not so difficult.

She found the Queen still bare-headed, playing petulantly with the pearls on her sleeves. Margaret looked about, her face heavy and pale. "Why, there you are, child," she said. "Comb my hair as it should be done. That woman pulls at it, though I have told her often. I will ask for some other." She looked with sudden helplessness at Angus' sister; she herself would not know how to begin ordering the Douglas women.

Jonet took the comb and ran it deftly through the rich hair. The Queen smiled, her full lips parting. "Ye have a gentle touch," she said. "How fortunate my lord Glamis will be in his wife! I dare say they will not call him Clang-Causey over long, with such a young lady awaiting him in his bed."

Jonet flushed. "The wedding is not yet, Madam." She found it, in fact, difficult to picture life other than at Tantallon. No doubt Glamis would not be very different, except that the Lyon writ would run before the Douglas. But she would see to it that her husband and her brother remained friends; anything else was fearful to think of.

"Glamis was not at Flodden," said the Queen.

"Madam, he had three uncles killed there."

"Well, you have found it all out. At any rate that's over now. I wish you well in your marriage, when it comes."

"Your Grace is gracious."

She said no more and combed on and thought how even the tocher was paid over now, so there could be no going back on the bridal. Beyond the veil of hair, the Queen was surveying her with close-set eyes. The child was more beautiful than oneself, not so much in feature—Margaret Tudor thought of herself as very handsome, with some reason still—as in an air about her, a certain sweetness of peace and calm. It was perhaps time Jonet Douglas went, helpful as she had been. Her Grace was almost certain Angus visited a mistress, and no doubt this chit knew it all. In any case a sister took attention from a wife.

"In life one gets back what one gives," said the Queen suddenly. "Fetch me my hat, the silk one."

Which hat? There were very many, hats, caps and wired veils in velvet and silk and lawn, heart-shaped and flat and hooded. There was a pair of sleeves stiffened with gold wire, and a great chain of red and white enamelled roses, and other beautiful things. Jonet had seen them often now but still liked to tidy them; everything was always tangled together. "Quickly," said Her Grace in impatience.

Jonet brought a hat over. "Not that; I think that after all I will wear the crimson hood."

It was a quarter-hour before a headdress was finally chosen. At last Her Grace was suited, but the bright colour she had selected showed her pale as a candle with pregnancy. Poor creature, thought the girl, she is never contented. Maybe the English are all so.

She watched the Queen, grandly dressed, descend the stairs at last. It was still possible to think of her as having had poems written to her by priest Wil Dunbar and bishop Gavin, one's uncle. Jonet knew his verses well, for they were read sometimes at Tantallon while the ladies sewed.

Great affairs called Angus often, and soon enough his royal wife clamoured to go back to her children and her comforts. There was no reason to stop her, and the cavalcade clattered off in a motley of banners with the farm-folk staring from their fields. The Douglas women gave a sigh of relief; they were rid of their demanding guest, and there should be no more to do now beyond everyday affairs except finish the altarcloth and make ready for Jonet's marriage. There was still much to do for that, although the shifts of fine linen were finished; but the wedding-gown itself was no more than a bolt of satin still, and would take much work to complete.

3

The May sunlight glistened on the sea and the Heads of Ayr rearing beyond. Everywhere was a deceptive calm. A ship sat in the bay with sails furled, surrounded by a swarm of small boats and waiting folk. In the cabin, a handsome bearded Frenchman prepared to land, his feelings mixed.

He had never met James IV, but that monarch had left it in his will that if any accident should befall himself while his son was still a minor, his cousin, John Stuart, Duke of Albany, should come to govern Scotland. Albany was not too willing, for all his interests as well as his delicate wife had had to be left behind in France. Yet he had heard, through his friend Antoine d'Arcy de la Beauté who had jousted with the late King and slept in his bed, that this was no longer a savage country but one full of scholars, poets and knights, with the arts and sciences far advanced; had not the King caused a man to fly on wings from the battlements of Stirling Castle? And they had tilted, in de la Beauté's time, for a black lady who sat in splendour in the high seat. Moreover, justice prevailed in the land, for the King saw to it himself.

Albany had heard the news of Flodden with grief, and a determination to hand on the King's country whole and prosperous to his son, in time. One's own affairs were of less importance; though he hoped to visit Agnès next year. She had wept on their parting, and assured herself that Albany's fastidious palate would be met with understanding in Scotland; in the ship's hold were spices and sugar as well as ammunition.

It had been a smooth crossing and now they scarcely rocked at anchor. Albany waited for the first of the small boats and then came out, for he was courteous, for the Scots nobles to kiss his hand.

They eyed him up and down; they were a rough lot. One or two attempted to address him in passable French; it was a second language here. Albany allowed himself and his body-servant to be lowered into the boat and rowed to land. He saw a seafaring town, studded with market-booths full of coloured stuffs in bales. Folk stared at his fine clothes and a woman in a coif came forward to finger them. Albany addressed her politely and she bobbed a curtsy; evidently he was a great lord, this son of James III's brother. He was not above speaking to common folk.

Later he met the little King. The women brought him in but with them was a gently-spoken young man in a flat cap of black velvet. His name was Davy Lindsay, and he had governed the child since James IV's time, by that King's wish.

Albany picked up the red-haired three-year-old boy and kissed him, in the French manner, once on each cheek. The child regarded him with secret eyes. Presently he said, flatly, "Ross is sick." The Duke set him down.

"Ross? He is your brozzer, *n'est-ce pas?* You are sad for him? Be of comfort, I have a gift for you." He signalled to his man; the fellow went out and returned with a brightly plumaged parrot, fresh from its cage, clinging to his fingers with dry claws. The little King stared, then smiled, holding out his arms. "She will talk to you," said Albany. "*Dis bon jour*, my friend."

"*Bon jour*," said the parrot. James V stroked her feathers. He did not show intense pleasure; he was wary of this stranger who spoke so oddly, although his clothes were beautiful. He was, however, pleased with his talking papingo; it would be more amusing than the company of Ross, who was only a baby and could not even say *bon jour*. It would pass the time till his mother came back. James V loved his mother.

The Queen herself received the Duke coyly, wearing a lawn scarf to hide her condition. She behaved as a woman may do with a handsome man; but her flirtations struck no spark. Albany had his own opinion of the Angus marriage and of the woman who had made it so soon. He would be civil to her, but keep watch. They exchanged formal courtesies and drank wine together, then Albany left to go to his apartments.

Margaret watched him go. She was fretful and discontented. The late King should have appointed nobody Regent except herself; it was a slight to her to have this Frenchman here at all. If he had responded to her it would have been different; but she was not at her most attractive, what woman would be? They said his wife, Agnès de la Tour, was a very great heiress. Strange when one reflected that this Albany's father had been a rebel against his brother James III and had escaped literally at a rope's end from this very castle, and won to France. He must have had smooth ways to be so greatly honoured there.

She cast about her restlessly; where was her husband? He left her alone more and more; it was that Traquair woman: he might as well have married *her*. If only she, Margaret, could take her sons and return to England! There, at Court, men of Albany's kind were daily met with, suave, courteous, worldly men; and there would be Harry, her brother whom she had not seen since he became King, and warm sunlit palaces, and the Thames flowing.

England. If only the coming child could be born there, away from this Albany and cold Scotland!

If she had known, Angus was having his own troubles with Janet of Traquair. Her child had been born, but she paid no more heed to it than if it had been a kitten. "Ye promised me, my fine lord, when ye gat me with bairn, that ye would wed me, that was after Flodden Field. And your Queen is no true wife, for a handfasting is a marriage." He knew it was true; in Scotland a promise to wed was binding. Her

Grace must never find this out: and he had scant leisure to devote to her. Who would watch her for him at the times when he must be elsewhere? Surely Jonet. Jonet's gentle ways would not offend the Queen and would ensure that the Angus interest did not fade in the fickle woman's heart. Jonet's own wedding must wait.

So Clang-Causey was written to to say he must bide awhile, and he was not too pleased, for he had accustomed himself to the thought of Jonet's beauty by now and was afire for it. He strode up and down in anger at Glamis, but could do little more. Jonet, on the other hand, was given scant time to pack her baggage; she must attend, by order of her brother, the Queen in Edinburgh.

She travelled there; and entered Her Grace's presence again. Margaret was sullen at first, and not too pleased to see her; then the old liking returned, for Jonet could make strangers of none. Before the week was out they were on the old pleasant footing, with the young girl combing the Queen's hair and sometimes playing with her at cards when there was no other diversion.

But Queen Margaret nourished a plan, and next time she was alone with her husband appealed to him, putting on a helpless air as she could do when she tried; and in fact was she not indeed helpless, a princess of England surrounded by strange folk? Within an hour she had made him agree to her plan; she would give Albany a wrong date for her lying-in, and when the closed chamber was being prepared would escape, her husband with her, and be over the Border before any looked for them. "And my sons will be better off at their uncle's Court; here they will grow up into savages. Be my friend in this, and my brother will reward you, never fear."

Angus did greatly fear. The more he thought of it, as the days went on, the less he liked it; to spirit the Scots King out of Scotland was too much, even for a Douglas. He would never be free of Tantallon again, perhaps never cross the Border again, if such a thing were laid to his blame. Yet reason told him to placate the Queen, let her think everything was as she wanted it, that the King and his brother would join them later; that was it. And Jonet should accompany them.

Jonet was told of it, secretly. Bewildered as she was at the plan to leave by night, she did as Angus told her; after all how could she question his orders? She helped wrap Her Grace in a great hooded cloak, and parcelled up certain of her valuables; and after it was dark she, Angus and the Queen crept out by way of the kitchens of Linlithgow, leaving the scullions sleeping by the fire.

The night outside was dark, with an autumn cold. Horses were waiting and they mounted. Jonet saw the Queen's unwieldy figure helped into the saddle; is she daft, the girl thought, to leave a warm bed in her state for such a ploy? But Angus was with them; it must be in order; he would know where to go and what to do.

It was some little time before the Queen's flight was discovered. The Regent thought she had gone into labour, and delicately refrained from asking, or intruding. By that time the fugitive party had gained the coast, and were riding south through mist and rain.

They drew rein first at Tantallon. Jonet saw the liveried men-at-arms and the red pile of the castle again with some relief; the Queen had not been well on the ride. Angus himself always seemed to grow in stature once in sight of his own walls, but it did not happen now. He showed Her Grace to her apartments, and drew Jonet aside. She looked up into his face, which had lost its confidence; he was like any harried man, uncertain of the future. He already regretted being a party to the Queen's flight, she was certain. But she would not question him.

Their mother was there, haggard and troubled as always since the death of her husband, the Master of Angus, at Flodden. Another old lady rode in, the Chamberlain's mother, Lady Hume, with her son's men. She was full of advice over the pregnancy and wearied the Queen and even Jonet. "One would think I had never borne children!" complained Margaret, glad when at last the Chamberlain's mother went home. Hume himself was to seize the King and his brother and bring them south. But the Regent Albany was watchful, and the plan failed.

The only real harm Albany and his men did the Queen was to seize old Lady Hume, still mouthing advice, and put her on a high-stepping nag and imprison her thereafter at Dunbar on bread and water. But Margaret Tudor was full of revenge. She left Tantallon, with her husband and Jonet, in haste when it appeared that Hume would not after all bring the royal children south; the flight was like a rout by now, and Her Grace had left her hats and jewels at Tantallon. She was not well; Jonet heard her complain about the pains as they rode. They spent a night at Coldstream, waiting fearfully for Henry VIII's writ to come so that they might cross the Border. The rain still drizzled down. Jonet stood at the narrow window to watch it, and reflected on what her brother had said to her; she was not happy about the journey, but must obey.

"Men will come with news for me; I must leave ye then, but will return." So he had said; but when to return, and how?

The Border lands were spongy with wet; their horses' hoofs sank in the ground, and the going was uneven. Now and again Jonet would ride over to succour the Queen. Her Grace was in a sorry state, an unwieldy, pain-racked woman in a sodden cloak, jogged by the ride.

"I can no more. I must have shelter. Find me a place." The labour had started, there was no doubt of that. Jonet rode forward in order to speak to the men. Her Grace must be housed wherever there was a roof, and swiftly; there was no more time.

A deserted peel-tower was visible among the wind and rain. Jonet rode back to the Queen. "Here is a place, my leddy. Ye will be safe here." God knew she doubted it; the English Lord Warden, Lord Dacre, had made ready the Scots Queen's welcome at Morpeth, further south.

They rode in below the tower. Dacre himself was there, full of anger and embarrassment; this was no place to receive the King of England's sister. "She may come in, but never a Scot with her," my lord vowed. He was a troubled man, dressed in a leather surcoat and ready for constant trouble, here on the Borders; the time was long gone when he had shared a barrel of green ginger with the dead King of Scots on justice-ayres. Already news of the Queen's escape had spread and it was rumoured that the young King was with her. Armed bands roved across the country, waiting for the kill. They had raided the dead at Flodden.

Jonet rode forward. "My lord, I am a Scot. Will ye not allow me in with Her Grace? She is in labour, and a woman's company is needful." The water-green eyes gazed up at the tired Lord Warden. Dacre, who had a soft heart when there was leisure, nodded. "You then, my lady; but none other."

They went in. Upstairs there was a straw pallet, and Her Grace lay down. She began to strain with the child and went on as dawn broke, as daylight came, as the noon sun later whitened. At last a small head was seen; it was delivered, not Angus' son, as he had hoped for, but a girl. Jonet cradled the child in her arms after its nose and mouth had been cleansed. The mother had no milk, and goat's milk mixed with water was brought. "Hush ye," crooned Jonet, occupied with my young Lady Margaret Douglas' crying.

"She must be christened," moaned the Queen, "lest worse befall." Jonet took the flaxen-haired child and made a sign on her forehead with water, as one could do if there were no priest. "In the name of the Father and the Son and the Holy Ghost, I baptize thee Margaret." She turned to the Queen and said, "Ye have borne a Christian soul."

"God be thanked," said the Queen. Her small eyes narrowed. "Send to my brother and say that Cardinal Wolsey is to be the child's godfather. He is more powerful in England than any man."

"I will do so." She told a horseman, and the baby slept. Margaret Douglas had made a grim entry into this world, nor would it be kind to her.

Angus knelt by the pallet and looked at his baby daughter. He was aware of a tug of protective affection; strange, when he had felt nothing for Janet of Traquair's child! But the tiny head, with its covering of silver-fair curls like snails' shells, diverted him. He needed diversion; the Queen his wife looked at him with fevered eyes full of reproach. What could he do that had not already been done? Arran and Hume were below, and between them they would sign a band against French Albany, and get the Queen back to her rightful place as Regent of Scotland.

He tried to say all this to her; but her cheeks were flushed and she seemed restless. Helpless, he signalled to Jonet, who sat nearby, nursing the baby. She came at once, with a caudle.

"Here is wine whey, my leddy." God knew how she had managed to procure it; outside the marauders still raged, my lord Dacre still called down curses on the Scots, and nothing could be seen for the drizzling rain. "I would go home, my lord," said the Queen, "to England." She did not seem to know that they were in England now.

"To Morpeth first, Madam, where my lady has all things prepared for ye."

"Has there been word from the King my brother?" The sick woman tossed on her pallet; why could she not have remained quiet at Linlithgow?

"Ay, there has been word; and from his Queen, who has sent ye comforts. They are waiting at Morpeth."

Morpeth. It was better furnished than here, and was where my lord and his lady abode always in the winter, here on the thankless Borders. The Queen closed her eyes. Angus did not know whether she had heeded him or not. He cast a final glance at Jonet and his daughter, then stole downstairs to sign the agreed band with Hume and Arran.

The Queen was borne to Morpeth, and promptly set that castle by the ears and, with her train, consumed all the provision set aside by Lady Dacre for the winter. Word came from King Henry VIII; she might travel south to him as soon as she could. His kind Spanish Queen sent a loving letter and, also, comforts for Her Grace and swaddlings for the little Margaret Douglas. Perhaps these had been intended for Catharine's own tragic children: and she also sent an easy pillion for Her Grace to ride. The child Margaret Douglas grew, and by the time they set out was able to have her fair curls tidy in a bonnet, riding before one of the servitors. Yet it was a draggle-tailed party, in no way resembling that with which the English Rose had long ago set forth from England. Even then Her Grace was full of tears, with reason; the news had come lately that the little Duke of Ross, her younger son by James IV, was dead.

"*He* will not be at peace till he has the King's life too." She blamed Albany.

Jonet tried to calm her. "Be at peace yourself, dear Madam; any man who wanted the crown would have killed the King as well. Yet he lives, to be your pride."

"Small pride or comfort have I: all have deserted me."

It was true, in a way; the Queen waited many hours at a named place for her husband Angus to join her, and escort her into England; but he did not come. Jonet cast her eyes down; Her Grace rode with mouth close-set, and bade the horses start.

After Northumberland was passed by with its marshes, England was green and fertile, with well-tended orchards and folk going about their business without fear. "May we never see Scotland again," said the Queen of Scots thankfully. "May we never see Scotland again!"

4

Jonet sat in England beside a worn-faced woman in a long gable hood, while the two fair-haired children, the Princess Mary and the Lady Margaret Douglas, played on the floor.

Jonet was sewing. There was always much to do in mending linen for the Queen of Scots, here at Greenwich. It was welcome enough in the company of Queen Catharine, who made her own husband's shirts. She was not engaged on one now but was gazing at the two children, her sad eyes lit with pleasure. Her fingers told her beads; Catharine of Aragon never left herself idle.

"They will grow up to be close friends, they are so near of an age," she said of the children. Jonet smiled, and agreed; but in herself she doubted if the Queen of Scots would be permitted to stay at her brother's Court indefinitely. The handsome young King, fresh from maying, had welcomed them at Blackheath when they rode down last May, after months of wintry hospitality from the much-put-upon Lady Dacre at Morpeth. That had been a grim time, with the Queen half dead and going from one bout of sickness to another; there had been a time when her life was despaired of, and that had beeen the day Angus chose to make known that he would on no account ride with them south. As always, Jonet saw his viewpoint; it was of no use to escape to England if his wife were dead. But royal Margaret had recovered and now wailed of her wrongs, a list of which she put to the Regent Albany's blame. As far as Jonet could judge, all that gentleman had done amiss was to order old Lady Hume to be put on the spirited horse and then in prison, which might indeed have been the death of her; but it was doubtful if Albany was as responsible as his men. Angus had stayed with the Humes, the Arrans, the Scots lords who thought of him as equal with them if not above them; down here he would only have been a hanger-on, the Scots Queen's husband. Jonet had not been unduly impressed with the brilliant, bejewelled Court of the young King Henry. There was much back-biting and casting down of eyes, and she had herself seen Queen Margaret walk in Greenwich gardens on the arm of the man who had killed her first husband, Norfolk of the grim mouth and cold hooded eyes, Margaret had known him, she said afterwards, from a girl; he had ridden north for her marriage to James IV. But he had become an enemy since then, and Jonet could hardly stomach the sight of the Queen on his arm, trailing among the courtiers who gossiped and whispered among the formal gardens by the river.

If she had known, Queen Catharine was saying her beads not too happily. She was well aware that since her own victorious command at the time of Flodden, while her husband was in France, Henry had cooled towards her. Before that he had looked at no other woman, but by now there was a kind of envy of her, a resentment, because, no doubt, she had been as successful a soldier as her mother, Isabella the Spanish Catholic, and had arranged for troops and transport and ammunition by way of York against the Scots. And after the victory all the bells in England had pealed for joy, and she, Catharine, had gone on a pilgrimage to Walsingham to thank Our Lady and to ask for the boon of a living child. Mary had been conceived then, on Harry's return home, and had lived, unlike the many dead children. But Catharine had seen the King's small eyes narrow and his mouth prim up in the way she dreaded, so out of keeping did it seem in the great pink handsome face. And since then, though he had lain with her, there was none of that gladness between them there had formerly been, ever since he had married her, his brother's wife, a young widow six years older than himself, as soon as his old father died and Harry became King and got his hands on much gold. The gold he had somewhat spent making war on France and Scotland, but there was still plenty of it left, and jewels; Catharine did not care for these, and her dress today was, as usual, plain. She glanced at the beautiful girl seated nearby. Would Harry ever glance at another woman? She should have more faith in him than that, and yet . . .

"Mama, Mama," said the Princess Mary, her little snub nose wrinkled in a smile. She staggered over to the Queen and pulled at her skirts. Catharine stroked the silver-fair hair. They were already talking of marriage for this child, to the Emperor.

"Bring Madge, your cousin." The Queen spoke low and softly, and Jonet Douglas turned her head. The Lady Margaret Douglas was still uncertain on her feet, and had to be helped across to her playmate. Jonet knew a sudden stab of anxiety for her brother's daughter; what would her life be?

There was the sound of a man's laughter and the King came in, flushed from tennis; his skin was so fair that it was said its hue could be seen to change beneath his fine lawn shirt when he was playing. He wore many jewels, as always, in especial a great ruby on his thumb. The small eyes scanned Jonet from their great height, but Henry spoke to the Queen, who had risen and they kissed one another.

"How fares my good Kate? And my pearl, how does she this day? Mary, come and kiss your father."

He swept Mary up into his great arms, and stood for a moment with the tiny child against his chest, both laughing with pleasure; Mary adored her father. Margaret Douglas stood watching them out of her blue eyes and her young aunt took her by the hand. The little creature must not be made to feel outcast because her own father and mother took small heed to her; Queen Margaret had gone today to sup with the Cardinal. Jonet smoothed the child's gown, which had belonged to her cousin who had outgrown it. The King's voice, high for so great a man, sounded above them.

"My niece Madge has a fair nurse. Why do ye not divert yourself at Court, Lady Jonet Douglas? Because your revered brother will not come to his wife is no reason for one so fair as yourself to hide under a bushel." He laughed at his own joke; Jonet regarded him steadily.

"Sire, I am loyal to my brother; he has been good to me. I beg of you to say nothing against him in my hearing."

"Why, he deserted my sister; done like a Scot, as I said then." The King's good nature had vanished and he wore the expression Catharine dreaded. He tried to regain his temper, however; this Scots girl was too lovesome to chide. For almost the first time in his life, he had taken heed of a woman other than his mother, long dead now, and his wife. He had never seen a beauty like that of Jonet Douglas; not fleshly, to weary a man after possession. It was a thing of the spirit, and it teased him to know her better. The King of England was not accustomed to teasing.

"We hunt tomorrow," he said, "in the woods about Beaulieu. Do you come, Kate, and bring my Lady Jonet to see how a hunt goes away." Women did not join in the sport, but would come to watch the baying hounds, with their great spiked and enamelled collars, loosed after the quarry, and the men ride off.

Jonet made her curtsy. If Queen Catharine went, she would accompany her. But she said no more, knowing she had only just failed to anger the English King. It was no service to Angus to make an enemy of his brother-in-law. She would obey in every courteous fashion, without losing her honour.

Beaulieu had been set aside as an establishment for the little Princess Mary, and the child and her cousin Madge—this was the name by which young Margaret Douglas came to be known—went there in a litter with her mother

the Queen, Jonet, and the nurses. They would stay now it
was summer, with the usual danger of the plague in
London. After the children had been taken away Jonet
stayed by the Queen. She had a love for devout Catharine,
though it was not hard to see that the King's affection for
his wife would not last long; the Queen took no trouble
with her appearance and spent all her waking time in
prayer, while other women danced and kept their eyes on
the King.

"I left gear in England when I was a bride; the jewels my
mother bespoke for me in her will." The Queen of Scots
used, once again, that old, forgotten claim; she would
never see the jewels, and both she and Cardinal Wolsey
knew it. But she would ask the Cardinal outright for
money, if it came to that; he was rich, and had had the
honour of being named godfather to her daughter. But he
looked at her with dull eyes; if she wanted money she must
work for it like other folk, King's sister or not.

"We will pay, Madam, for any news sent out of
Scotland."

Margaret's full lips fell apart. "But I will not return
there," she said. How could she do so, after the welcome
here, and sitting on a dais with Harry's wife and their
younger sister Mary, Queen of France, surrounded by red
and white roses and pomegranates, for all their royal
arms? Scotland was an unwelcome memory of wind and
rain and bog. But the heavy head of the butcher's son—so
she thought of him, to give her mind calm—shook slowly
in its red hat. All of Wolsey's movements were ponderous,
as if power weighed him down. He spoke deliberately,
assessing each word.

"Madam, your jointure, your lands and castles, are all in
the north, none in England. It is advisable to return soon to
claim them, else they will be lost to your warring nobles."

"They are warring against the Regent Albany, not
myself," said Margaret spitefully. She let her mouth droop

again. "I have no money," she said, and tears of self-pity
rose; he took no heed of them. "Surely," he said, "the late
King left you silver."

"None." She was lying, and he knew it. James IV had
left her entrusted with a box containing eighteen
thousand great French crowns of the sun, in trust for his
boy. Margaret had spent it, she could not remember how.

Wolsey hid his contempt; this woman might still have
her uses. "I will," he said, "arrange so much," and he
named a small sum. "We will be glad of news," he told her
again.

No more than that? He could supply all I want and never
feel it, thought Margaret. Her mind began to run about
like a frightened thing. To return to that land of rocks and
storms, to the roughness of Angus, the treacherous
smoothness of Albany, and so poor that she could bribe no
one? How much more welcome it would be to retire to some
palace here in the shires, and sometimes come to Court,
and there would be Harry playing his lute and dancing
elegantly, and compliments from the courtiers on the
lasting bloom of her own beauty! She was well, rested,
better by far than when she had come. And the children,
Madge and her remaining son the King of Scots, must
somehow be brought to her.

"You need have no fear but that we will pay for private
news, Madam." The Queen of Scots was of no more value
than that; and unless the Regent Albany were more
foolish than folk said, there would be nothing of great
importance to send. This importuning woman must go
back whence she came.

"Can you let me have nothing now? I am penniless, my
lord Cardinal." She raised the tear-filled, pleading eyes to
him; out of embarrassment he handed her some silver, and
promised more soon. Margaret almost flounced out of his
presence. So much for the godfather of her daughter! And
she, whose mother had been a royal princess of the house of
York, to have to take money like a beggar from a man

whose father had hacked meat in London!

Harry himself would give her nothing more, she knew. Last time she had pled with him he had flushed scarlet above his short golden beard, grumped some excuse and turned his broad back. He was putting on flesh a little. It was unfair. Their father had died leaving the richest coffers in Europe, and Harry, from being an eager, strictly brought-up lad of eighteen had spent it all on himself and his Field of the Cloth of Gold where Kate and Queen Claude of France had ended by having to pull their infuriated husbands apart by their coats. "Nobody wants to aid a widow woman," Margaret told herself; then remembered that she was married again. She had forgotten Angus on this visit, and it seemed as if he had forgotten her also; which was a blessing. His sister was still about her, and no doubt sent spying reports to the north. The girl was sly, and one must watch her.

Nearby, at Richmond, an embalmed dead body lay, its red hair dulled with dust. Henry VIII had refused his Scots rival Christian burial because James IV had been excommunicated by the Pope for aiding the French at the time of Flodden. By now Henry had forgotten about the matter. He himself had lately received the Pope's Golden Rose for preserving Christendom. He was well spoken of abroad; they had lit bonfires for joy in Venice when the news came that the Scots were beaten at Flodden.

The Queen of Scots did not ask about the body of her husband: she had forgotten also. Querulous and complaining, she made ready at last to ride back north; and Jonet Douglas with her.

Jonet was glad to go. Not only had her wedding to Glamis been delayed, but she had her own troubles with the King of England. He had come one day when she was out walking with the children and their nurse, and had sent the others away, firmly taking Jonet's hand and placing it on his arm. She could feel beneath her fingers the stiff satin and raised brocade; it was more real to her than what Henry was saying, and in fact, at first, she could not believe her ears.

"A grievous thing has happened to me," he began. "I had not thought it would happen; I have been married these seven or eight years and am faithful to my wife. But your beauty has opened my eyes to a thousand desires. We would have you always with us, in some position about the Queen; that way my heart will be glad, and I may see you daily."

She did not think he was asking her to be his leman; all his words spoke only of honourable love, to be able to watch and gaze. But she could not consider that. She withdrew her hand gently from his arm.

"Sire, I am a Scot, and my duty lies there, with my betrothed husband. He has waited long to wed me, and I will not disappoint him."

"Any man who wins you is lucky. A Scot! You are over fair to be one of that race; they cannot keep their word from one day to the next, but suit their pockets always." He gloomed, turning his great head away from her in its plumed bejewelled hat. She had seen the quick colour spring up in his face and knew she had not pleased him; but how could one do so without dishonour? He was like a spoilt child, avid for what he wanted, considering no one else. Yet he was a King and could, no doubt, confine her in prison or a convent if she did not do his will. Something held her back and gave her courage. She raised her eyes to him.

"You speak much ill of the Scots, Sire. It is not a rich country and the folk are not like your folk. We and the English do not deal well together, maybe, despite all friendship, because we see things in a different manner; sometimes we foresee, not yet seeing. We laugh and weep differently. But to say a Scot has no honour is untrue. We have our knaves, as you have; but do not make their shame cover us all."

He stared at her, the small eyes assessing her, standing there proud, clear-eyed, unyielding. He was not yet certain of himself: the man he was to become would have had her in prison. He turned on his heel and flung away, towards the Queen's apartments. She will comfort him like a mother, Jonet told herself. She hurried after the nurse and the children, trembling a little. She would be thankful to get out of rich, perilous, greedy England, and go home.

Much later, she heard among other things that King Henry VIII had at last taken a mistress, Elizabeth Talboys, whom Janet had met at Court: and Bess bore him a living son.

5

The journey back to Scotland was uneventful, Her Grace in much the same ill-temper as when she had ridden south. Jonet saw the hills and rough grey walls of Cumberland at last with joy; her cheeks were flushed with pleasure and the cold air. Queen Margaret looked at her suspiciously.

"I believe you do not regret leaving England," she said, her eyes hard; she had been silent on the journey, and Jonet knew that she herself was no longer trusted, being a Douglas. She smiled. "Indeed, Madam, I am blithe to be back in my own country." The very air was different, sharper, challenging; there was no softness here, no fine palaces. The horses' hoofs squelched through moss and mud in a dour silence. Jonet was glad to be almost home. Soon now they would come to the Border, and maybe meet trouble there; yet Jonet would not have turned back for much gold. Her heart beat faster; she wished the horses would fly with the wind. Suddenly she gave a cry. "Madam, Madam, my brother's men are here!" For she could see a brightness against the grey sky, the crowned heart banner itself; Angus and his men rode towards them. She knew then that, through one bog and another, they must be already in Scotland; Angus would never cross the Border in force.

He looked grimmer, older; he had grown a short beard, which changed him. He louted down and kissed his royal wife's hand, then turned to Jonet, giving her a great hug. "I am blithe to see ye," he murmured. "John Glamis grows impatient. He says he has waited over long."

"Why, so he has done," replied Jonet reasonably. She had almost forgotten her own wedding in the toils there had been. She would have announced her willingness to

let the ceremony take place as soon as might be, but Angus
frowned, and waved aside the matter. "I have a house in
Edinburgh," he said, "where ye may bide meantime." He
had kissed the child Madge, riding in her mother's litter
and staring placidly with calm eyes at the bearded
stranger. She had travelled well, giving no trouble; indeed
she was the quietest child Jonet had ever known. Perhaps
too much change, the going from place to place and
meeting many folk, had accustomed Madge to insecurity,
even so young.

The house in Edinburgh looked on to the street, with its
constant traffic and smell of road-middens. The Queen
complained day and night and asked why she could not go
to Holyrood? It was more comfortable there, and pleasant,
for James IV had had plaster spread on the walls for her
first coming, all painted with swags of flowers. But Angus
made one excuse after another, and Jonet came to see that
he did not want the Queen to meet with Regent Albany,
who was rumoured to be about to return again from
France. She herself took the days as they came, waiting for
her own affairs to be concluded; she acknowledged that she
was in no hurry to wed John Glamis. There had been so
much to recall, and she was again near her brother, which
made her happy; and looking after little Madge Douglas
was a pleasure, as the child's mother paid small heed to
her. The Queen was more anxious about her son the King
of Scots, and had been allowed to embrace him, and found
him grown.

The Queen no longer wanted Jonet about her, as she had
grown suspicious of all Angus' kin. The girl was escorted
back to Tantallon to prepare for her wedding.

It was good to be home, and to feel her mother's arms
about her. "As God sees me, daughter, ye are the more fair
since going into England. Alison will be coming over to
hear of all the English fashions that the ladies wear. Since

gaun to Wedderburn she is grandly dressed and thinks no one can equal her."

Elizabeth Douglas smiled, showing teeth which were still good despite bearing many children. She had been a beautiful woman like her Drummond sisters, but her hair now was grey. She showed Jonet the wedding dress, which had not progressed during the time in England as they had been sewing at other things. It would be beautiful, but there was work still to be done on it. "They tell me Queen Catharine is a notable needlewoman. Maybe she showed ye the stitches she uses."

"Mother, she does fair black stitching on white cloth, but I do not want black on my wedding gown."

The gown was of pale satin, embellished with tiny pearls from the Scots river Tay. Day after day the sisters and their mother stitched at it, and at last the time had come when it was ready, and the bridegroom coming south.

"I would your father were here to give ye away. Angus is busied with his great affairs, so it will have to be George."

Jonet tried to remember her father. When she was a little child he had been there, gruff and seldom spoken, but when he spoke it was to effect. There had been a legend drifted back from Flodden; the Master of Angus had mocked James IV because, having come down from the high place where they would have won the fight, the King had ridden out in full heraldic panoply. "Ye take no risk," sneered the Master, "fighting in full coat-armour and royal cognizance." And James IV, stung, had said, "Ye will see me fight without either," and had stripped off his bright-coloured tabard and helm and put on a plain coat, in which he had gone to his death a lance's length from the Earl of Surrey. And Jonet's father had been killed close behind him, with many of the lords of Scotland. Elizabeth Douglas' eyes misted over.

"I was married twice," she said, "but never again. After your father died I craved no other man."

I crave no man at all, thought Jonet. Within herself she
was somewhat frightened and shy at her coming wedding
to Glamis, whom she remembered as not gentle. It was
true that she had denied Henry VIII of England his desire,
but in a way the English King had been like an uncertain
boy. From what Jonet remembered of John Lyon he was
certain in his ways, and rough. She prayed for a better
understanding of him. More than anything she asked to
become a good wife, and the mother of living children. The
spectacle of Angus' failing marriage had not encouraged
her.

There was much she heard, then and later, about affairs in
Edinburgh. The Queen was said to be showing too much
favour to Arran, that loose-mouthed seducer, the King's
kin, who had in his time lost the Scots navy for James IV
and the *Great Michael*, that largest ship ever built. Also
Her Grace encouraged the Earl of Lennox, a smooth-
spoken man who was a favourite of the little King, having
sons of his own. Jonet heard all of it, feeling as if it
happened in another world; it hardly seemed possible to
her now, as one day followed another, that she could have
been with Her Grace at the birth of her daughter, and
ridden with both of them south.

Her Grace would not be at the wedding, any more than
her husband. They had greater matters in mind than the
giving away of a Douglas bride, although half the land
spoke of that. But there were other things to speak of,
notably the way the Queen's friends had ridden off, not
liking Angus' way with them. From having reviled him,
men began to cry out again for the Regent Albany, who
was with his sick wife in France. There was a feeling of
uncertainty, of danger, as if war cast its shadow. But with
whom were they to war if not England? And the time was
not ripe for that.

Violence broke out at the end of April, with a fitful wind
laying flat the flames of street-torches that burned all

night into the morning. They flickered across the glimmer of swords, drawn with a hiss in the capital's streets, the cinquefoils of Arran brandished against the crowned heart banners. Shouting and skirmishing continued as Arran, Warden of the East March, was chased out of Edinburgh by Angus' men. As for Her Grace, she sided with the losing party and wept because her friends had fled. "I ken *my* friends," Angus said, and forced his way into his wife's presence and wrested the child, Madge Douglas, from her. The little creature came unprotesting; she was used enough to be the cause of strife. "Our only comfort in this marriage has been the child," wailed the Queen. "Do not take her away from us."

But Madge Douglas was taken, and delivered to Tantallon. Once there, she was served by Douglas ladies; but her young Aunt Jonet was soon to leave her for Glamis.

There was another fight, less famous, a few weeks later, when Arran tried to re-enter Edinburgh. He had been, they said, to France to bring back the Regent. Meantime, the Regent's friend, Antoine d'Arcy de la Beauté, was murdered by the Hamiltons in a bog.

And the Regent returned.

6

Clang-Causey rode down for his marriage in company with a great clangour of armed men, a priest with them: he said he would not trust a Douglas to get him wed. That clan exchanged angry looks with one another and the men clapped their hands to their sword-hilts; but no action was taken, for Angus needed Glamis' friendship in the north.

Jonet was dressed in her finery, and came on the arm of George her brother to the altar. In that moment, beside her bridegroom dressed in a rich doublet, she was aware of all her kin; her mother, her once fair face lined with child-bearing and sorrow; busy Alison and her husband Hume of Blackadder; George's Isobel, proud of herself as the heiress of Pittendriech who would be one of the Glamis' neighbours. And her unmarried sisters were behind her, as attendants, almost as fine as she was herself. Clang-Causey's heavy face lightened as they exchanged vows and rings together. He had had a private word long since that Jonet Douglas was well instructed in housewifely duties, which would make for comfort at Glamis. If she would likewise forget she was a Douglas, and obey him, all might be well.

That was the matter almost done with except for receiving the Host, which all of the company did, from the hands of William, prior of Coldinghame, their brother, and the gentle-faced priest who had ridden down with the bridegroom, whose name was also John Lyon. Among them, close to the groom, there stood a thin man of medium height, not notable, and with sharp features and a whining voice. His name was William Lyon and he looked on the bride with envy. If fortune had granted him so fair a young woman to take to his bed, ne would be thankful. But his lot was less well set out than his lord's. He made a grudge of it, reminding himself of it all through the night, after which the wedding-party would return to Glamis on the morrow.

After the feasting the couple were bedded. Jonet's mother and sisters had undressed and kissed her and combed out her hair. The men brought in Glamis, still silent and curt as he had been since coming here. The Douglases noted it, and left with angry looks. It was no pride to them to have wedded their fairest kinswoman to a boor. But Angus had said the match was advisable.

Jonet lay in bed, her head turned towards her husband; she felt his hostility, and for some reason pitied him. It was not good for any man to be so at odds with everyone. She turned her eyes away for a moment and surveyed the grand coverlet and the tester, bearing the Douglas device and its crest, a salamander in flames. The gold thread in the embroidery gleamed in the light of the candle. Glamis reached over with his thick fingers, and put the latter out. He was pleased enough; and would the more readily take his bride if he could no longer see her beauty, the bright hair shining on the pillow, her water-green eyes, gentle and proud, and her fearlessness. A Douglas woman was maybe unchaste for all of that. He began to fumble at her; if there was no virginity he would complain on the morrow. He knew he should talk with her, cozen her, first: but could think of nothing comfortable to say. Tomorrow her hair, whose softness he could feel against him now, would be twisted up under the round hood of a wife; that would become her. He thought of it but could not say it; anything he said would be blustering and forthright and he had best keep silence. He had never before felt the need.

Jonet received him gently. Soon he thought of a thing to say. "The journey to Glamis will be hard going, with the roads sunk in mud all the way to Forfar."

"I do not know those parts, my lord. Ye must show them

to me."

How proud he would be, he thought, escorting this beauty! The folk would be out on the roads to see her and her train ride by. He began to think of the tenants at home, of the low thatched hovels and a scraping of ground covered in cabbages or oats by summer. In the winter snow would cover them completely, and no one could have found them, often, except for the black smoke coming up from the chimneys through the snow. He got on well enough with poor folk. It was only these Douglases, cocksure of themselves . . . He felt his wife move against him. She had been a virgin. He was pleased.

Jonet lay with eyes shut, feeling the new hurt in her body. Already it saddened her to be leaving the south with this man, the green Border lands soaked by mist and rain. At Glamis it would be cold, her mother had told her. But there would be new things there; she would take pride in being a housewife. It was something to have her own place, not, any more, to be ordered, except by her husband. Perhaps he would not always be at home. She made herself hold to her pity for him, constantly overcoming dislike. She spoke to him; her voice was low and pleasant, saying some ordinary thing. But it broke his silence.

"Ye kenned naught of love in England," he told her. She smiled against him; what would he say if she told him about King Henry? But she only said, "No, my lord. Did ye think to blame me for the knowing? I knew I was to be your wife, and listened to no other."

"All the grand places and folk . . . I thought maybe . . ."

"No. I do not need grand folk."

"Glamis is grand enough," he said defensively. "We have twelve silver flagons of seven pounds' weight each one."

"They will be kept shining, never fear."

"That will be comfortable, and all of it . . . Jonet lass . . ."

He took her again, wordlessly. After that it was more at ease between them. Jonet lay still. She had heard her husband grunt at last with satisfaction, a deep male sound; casting back in her mind she remembered her grandfather, old Bell-the-Cat, who used to take her on his knee and let her play with his great beard, to grunt just so. It was not so hard to please men.

She looked at John Glamis in the dawn as he still slept, at the heavy face which had seemed so brutal, but was at the least honest; his hands, which possessing her had been hard as leather, lay inside the sheet. It was better to be married to such a man than to . . . William Lyon. What had made her think of that one, or of anything except that her arms showed bruises now in the daylight? She knew nothing of William Lyon; she put him out of her mind.

The farewell to Tantallon was accompanied with great noise by Alison, who had bustled about so much yesterday that she might have been the bride. As they made ready to go she burst into tears. "My sister, it will be long ere we meet again! I would ye werena going so far."

"Fear not, we will meet maybe at Pittendriech, or at our Uncle John's at Innerpeffray." That was a half-way house; they would rest there tonight, and Uncle John Drummond the younger rode in the train with them, grey-haired now but still active, having kissed their mother farewell.

"Hume will not let me go to Innerpeffray," wailed Alison. Jonet smiled, for Alison's husband Hume of Blackadder was a quiet little man and seemingly under his wife's thumb. It was true that Alison was forever to and fro in other folk's houses, and maybe Hume had put his foot down about that. "We will meet again," she told Alison, "never fear."

John Glamis had said nothing. He was thankful to get his wife and the serving-men out on the road north. He rode a grey horse, Jonet a cream-coloured palfrey; above them the bright banners waved, the azure lion crossed with the crowned heart; the women had made them ready over the months, and no thieves or robbers would dare attack so well-found an assembly. The man William Lyon rode close, his sword at his side, like the rest.

Jonet fought back tears herself as they set off. She did not look back towards rose-red Tantallon, fearing that to show her grief might anger her husband. Instead, on the ride, she remembered many homely things she had taken for granted day after day; young Margaret Douglas with her flaxen hair and quiet child's ways; old Uncle Kilspindie and his raucous townswoman of a wife, who ruled him utterly. And the constant sound of the sea, crying night and day beneath the walls. At Glamis there would be no sea.

"Tell me of Glamis," she said to her husband when they were alone that night, after the great welcome at Innerpeffray. John Lyon turned to her; by now he was deep in love; how gracefully she had ridden beside him on the palfrey, all day, and made no complaint about the mire that muddied her skirts! He would try to say anything which would please her. He answered slowly. "It is a mighty place. It is one of the four great fortresses of the north. There is Cossins, Glen Ogilvy, Doonan and Glamis, but Glamis is the greatest. Once it was the palace of kings. A king died there. They say he was murdered."

"But now it will be our home."

"Ay."

She was thinking how she would order the maids and make the place warm with wood fires when it was cold; and there would be the housekeeping and brewing and baking, all to be done no doubt by the women; but a bride who did not keep an eye on her servants lost their respect and they would cheat her. So her mother had told her, and her mother was wise enough. She would be prudent, go slowly at first, make them love her, then they would do everything as it should be done. She wondered if many of them were bastard Lyons as the servants at home were mostly bastard Douglases. She did not ask Clang-Causey; he might be offended. But he was gentler that night with her than he had been; she was glad of it, and sensed a change in him. The biggest change, after all, was marriage; and she was able to contrive soft answers to Glamis, though she did not love him.

William Lyon, riding in his own place behind them, was busy with a fantasy. He told himself that Jonet Douglas was his bride, that he had possessed her these past nights. It was like the day of her wedding, when he had drunk deeper and deeper of wine after beholding her fair beauty brought to the altar to be married to that boor, his lord. Now, in his mind, her fair breasts lay naked beneath his hands, her mouth lay open to receive his kiss, his fingers caressed her long hair. He watched her out of the corners of his eyes as they rode; it gave him pleasure to have, as it were, a secret assignation with her. Despite her proud blood, it was as though he took a hostage home. Day after day, at Glamis, he could watch her; and dig into his mind for the rest. No doubt when they met day after day she would speak a word to him, give him reality other than the stuff of dreams. He would become her right-hand man on whom to call, he told himself; he, William Lyon, with no woman of his own, no child, nothing but a few bare acres by gracious consent of his lord. He knew Clang-Causey's ways and when he would be from home, busied about the estate or with such matters as his gross mind thought of importance. He, William, and my Lady Glamis would not be strangers by then. And maybe ... some day ... Meantime, he would hide away every word she dropped him in carelessness, remember every look on her fair face and in her eyes; and savour them to himself as he lay alone.

Jonet had her own reward when she saw the keep of Glamis rise like a fairy's castle out of the sunlit plain. They had entered a new country; once the Perthshire hills were left behind, fields changed to dark woods, part-ploughed land. At last there had been a few flat miles, with humped mountains in the distance whose shapes she did not know. She was sore with long riding in the saddle, and shifted restlessly. But the towers! They were like the colour in the heart of a pale rose, open to the day.

"It will not be far now," said Clang-Causey.

He had shed some of his dour silence and bullying ways on the journey, and had told her, with some satisfaction, that she could be proud to be the lady of Glamis. He discoursed again, having found a subject, on the king who had died there.

"He was Malcolm II, far back. His murderers they say were drowned crossing the frozen loch, but the ice gave under them. He had been used to hunt on the hill. That was where they meant to build the castle, but every night the stanes were cast down, and found in the morning, and in the end there was a dream had. *Build the castle in the bog / Where 'twill neither shak' nor shog*. It was the fairies didna like it on their hill; at least, so they say." He had finished what was a long speech for him; he had flushed, and the hot eyes raked her. She turned a smiling face to him.

"It is a fair place," she said. "I will try to keep it worthily."

"Ye may well do so. It is the greatest house in these parts. The Douglas writ does not run here. Remember it."

She felt a slight resentment rise. "My brothers have land nearby. They would be your good neighbours if ye would be theirs."

He bridled. "And who is to say that I am not a good neighbour? Folk get as good as they give."

"Some folk give nothing," she heard herself saying.

"May we both keep God's peace."

"We are well enough kent of God. We have St. Fergus here and St. Donald, and his nine daughters who are buried beneath an oak."

She laughed. "He was no saint if he had nine daughters."

"Say ye so?" But they were riding into Glamis, contained in its high wall. She forgot everything in exclaiming at its beauty, and he was pleased.

Afterwards she remembered many things. Clang-Causey had carried her in his arms below a stone lintel into a great arched hall. There the servants waited, ready to greet their new lady. Clang-Causey's lively old mother Lady Huntly was there, in scarlet hose to show off her neat ankles. Some of the galaxy of aunts were with her, mostly in old-fashioned netted cauls. Jonet could not remember their names at first, but they had married all over the county and beyond; Lady Erroll, Lady Hay, Lady Lovat, Lady Rhynd, Lady Ochterlony. But one thing she remembered above all the rest. Glamis strode past the chattering concourse of women to where a tall quiet serving-man waited, and brought him to her.

"This is Patrick Charteris of Cuthilgurdy, my faithful man. Ye may commend him to anything and trust him in the carrying out if it."

She extended her hand gladly to the good servant. Behind him she saw, and had sensed them all through the journey, the unwavering eyes of William Lyon, with their pale stare. Why did she dwell on him so, among all these welcoming folk? He had done her no harm. She must not be foolish. She turned to Lady Huntly her mother-in-law, and received her warm kiss, and that of the rest.

Meantime, Angus and his brother George sat drinking in a tavern in Edinburgh, despite the Regent's request that they leave the town. Angus was morose, turning his whisky-quaich about in his fingers. He would not tell George, for fear of being thought foolish, what was troubling him; the lack of Jonet's fair face at Tantallon. He had no comfort nowadays from the Queen his wife, and had used to like to ride down to visit his small daughter alone, but last time Madge had curtsied stiffly, and had not run to him. In former times her young aunt had been there, and would say smiling, "Run, Madge, run! It is my lord your father!" And the child's blue eyes would light up from their usual blankness, and Madge would come stumbling into his arms, and he would lout down and kiss her hand because she was, when all was said, a princess of England, being a queen's daughter. But now there were plenty to remind Madge of her state, and none to remember that she was still a child. He himself must take more heed to her. If only Jonet were not so far away in the north!

He sipped his whisky; already it had made his head fuddled, and he heard George, who was in a like state, speak indistinctly. He was speaking of the Regent, newly returned to Scotland. Angus scowled. His own royal wife had given the Frenchman over sweet a welcome, as he had feared she would.

"They say," he replied, as though denying something, "that he doesna like leaving his lady-wife sick in her tower, La Tour; de la Tour d'Auvergne; that was her name."

"Tell that to bonnie Jean Abernethy," said George. "They say she's borne the Regent a bairn, and he treats it like a princess." He had no illusions about women: he was glad to be free of his own wife's tongue, for the time.

"Maybe." Angus was not interested. He began to mouth his grudges, scarcely any longer knowing where he was. George, who as a rule was cautious and practical, had the fumes in his head likewise; he hardly listened, nor did either of them notice a dark man slip up to the landlord, and give him silver.

"Again!" The next tankard was not as good as the first; but they were full. They cursed, yet drank it; said more about Albany and damned him and his ancestors, and then slept, nodding over the table. The landlord approached and closed the shutters. What followed was not for day-by-day customers to witness, and he had been paid well enough.

Angus awoke to a pain in his head, and a strictness about his wrists where they were bound together. It was a fine day and the sea sparkled. The sea? Tantallon? But they were on a ship: it rocked at anchor.

"I can hear French spoken," he heard George say. He struggled up, swearing at the tight bands still about his wrists. They must have been out cold with the whisky; he remembered nothing since the tavern. They might have been dead, or thrown in prison. But they were safe, and somehow in France.

"We have slept over long," grunted George. He had worked free of his bonds and sat up rubbing his sore head. Presently he came and undid his brother's ropes—they had been loosely enough put on—while a trampling of feet came from overhead, on the deck.

"It is Albany and my royal wife who have done this," grunted Angus. "They would be free of us." He felt a fool, but recognised the warning. Next time it would not be so merciful; they had best stay here awhile.

"They have taken Arran's part," grumbled George.

"Ay."

A flicker of rebellion died; if they went back, who would dare receive them? Tantallon would be guarded, and Jonet was far north. George thumped a fist on the bulwark, the blood returning to his wrists. "It was nae guid marriage ye made," he told Angus. The latter shrugged.

"Where are we to go now?" asked George. But the

fecund imagination of my lord of Angus was blank for the time; he was still occupied with the implied insult of the thing. He, the Queen's husband, to be sent drugged out of the country! She must have known and approved it. No doubt Albany was her lover.

But they received the answer soon; all plans had been carefully laid. A personage appeared with a letter; it was from the Regent. Angus opened and read it, then gave a snort of angry laughter.

"It is courteous enough," he said. "The good soul is a diplomat. I—we—are appointed ambassadors to the King here. I doubt Francis will have been informed of this journey."

"Maybe, and maybe not," said George. "But keep the letter."

"Ay. Have we money? We should ride to Blois."

They both had what they had left with, and more was given them in French crowns. They got ashore, found horses and direction, and rode off with as much dignity as they might. Angus hid his continuing rage. The Regent's letter at least saved their faces. He and George might sojourn here in fair France as long as they liked; and it would be blithesome to be far from the Queen. She had wearied him for long. Let her go to her whoredoms with Arran and Albany; he had young Madge to prove the marriage. He would write to Tantallon, and to Glamis. There was much to do to arrange his life.

They rode a day's journey, then stopped at a tavern where the beds were clean, but the wine watered. Angus saved his face by loud complaint; the landlord concluded that these travellers were notable seigneurs, and gave them better wine made in the region.

"It is a pleasant enough country," said Angus presently. George nodded. "Ay," he said, "and let affairs in Edinburgh stew in their own juice. We have left them; now let them manage for themselves." From his way of speaking anyone would have been certain that Scotland's fate depended on their presence. They pledged one another in more wine, then went to bed and slept well.

They went to a tailor, and bought fine clothes; they would ruffle it at King François' Court, which was said to be a gay one. The Queen of Scots' husband was a Douglas, not nobody; and Angus fancied his own appearance in a French ruff.

It was all very well, for the time. But Henry VIII was angered over the whole business, for it made his sister look a fool as well as the men. He gave out one of his increasingly arbitrary commands; no Scot was to be permitted to remain in England, but should make his way home instantly, with a white cross marked on his garments. "Done like a Scot!" became the King's oath for anything troublesome. But the Queen's husband diverted himself at Blois, out of range of England's anger.

Back in Edinburgh, the returned Regent Albany looked once again out of the window at the blue line of Forth which could be seen from the Castle on its height. He congratulated himself on having rid Scotland, for the time, of the Queen's husband. There was one less focus now for discontent, for plotting against him and causing brawls in the streets. He wished that he had someone in whom to confide; dead Antoine de la Beauté, murdered barbarously, would have listened, would have made intelligent suggestions as to how to proceed now. Albany blamed himself for having sent Antoine over to so lawless a land while he himself was with his dying wife in France. It was unlikely that Agnès would recover. She had given him no children and he had not revealed to her his brief affair with young Jean Abernethy, nor the existence of the child Eléonore whom he loved. He would have Eléonore reared in France, not here. But Agnès de la Tour d'Auvergne he loved for herself, not only for her gold and broad acres of Lauragais and Douzenac; and while he fulfilled his promise to dead James IV to guard this kingdom for the child King, he could not be with his wife; she would die at once in this cold unwelcoming air. But he must do his duty; and when he was angry fling his bonnet on the fire, which he would sometimes do to relieve his feelings.

So much chaos, in no way resembling the late King's civilised Court when Scotland had been one of the foremost countries in the Renaissance! Music, poetry, jousting, surgery, all these had flourished here; now there was only fighting and murder. *Woe to the land whose King is a child.* Albany was aware that many of the nobility resented him and would go out of their way to make his task well-nigh impossible. It would have been different, woman though she was, if Queen Margaret had proved worthy to hold the land for her son the King. But she was concerned only with her passions, which lately had included himself. He disliked her, but it was not politic to make the fact evident. Now that her husband had been packed off overseas there would be no limit to her coy flirtation. He would take it so far and no further; the woman must not be offended, or all was lost. Her son loved her; Albany had tried to awaken affection in the boy for himself, but he was not certain that he had won it.

He turned, went to the door and called a servant. "I would see His Grace the King."

Presently the red-haired child appeared, his mother leading him by the hand. Albany downed his irritation; he had wanted to talk to James alone. The little boy had the papingo on his wrist; it was with him always, bright of feathers, imitating everyone, diverting the lonely child. He spoke now, lifting his face to the Frenchman after his mother had had her hand kissed. "She can whistle," he said, "like a blackbird, and hoot like an owl. Davy Lindsay taught her. He has written a poem."

The Queen shrugged. "Maybe my son needs other tutors," she said. Her eyes roved over Albany; so handsome a man, and they said his wife would not live, although she had hung on over the years in an inconvenient fashion. If only ... perhaps, if the Angus marriage could be done away with, knowing Angus to have been contracted first to that woman, Janet of Traquair ...

Albany had held out his hand to the King. "Ye have spoken of the bird, Your Grace, but not of yourself, " he said in halting Scots. "Are ye well? And happy, and learning fast from Monsieur Davy?"

"Sir, he is teaching me French."

"Speak some to me." Albany had led the Queen to sit down among cushions near the window. Outside the sky was grey. James V shook his head, and went and hid his face against his mother's skirts. She stroked the red hair absently, her gaze on Albany.

"He has grown, since your last coming, my lord, has he not?" Her French was rusty, but he answered her in the same language.

"Indeed; soon he will be a man, the months fly so fast." He turned to the Queen, his well-kept hands outspread in pleading. "Madame, I would speak with ye regarding his guardianship. The time will come when I must return to France, where my wife is ill."

Margaret pouted. "But ye are his guardian by the will of the late King. Do not desert us now." She looked down at her hands, and at the King's head against her lap. "My husband Angus may return once ye go," she said. "He cares for naught but himself and his family. The Douglases would seize power if they could; and there is nobody but myself, if you are not here, to prevent it. Indeed I do not know how I could do so alone." She raised a pleading face to him. She was still handsome, and knew that she could as a rule move him by a show of weakness. But he ignored her plea, and spoke again.

"I have been thinking that we could elect a list of lords who would have a care to him, each in his turn. I have in mind Lennox, Arran, perhaps even your husband by the end. Youth is his fault; when he is older he will be wiser."

"I love my lord Lennox," said the King suddenly, raising his head, the small pale oval face and dark eyes thoughtful. Lord Lennox always spoke to him as if he were a man; he had two sons of his own and James throve on stories of them. A life in charge of my lord Lennox would be pleasant. But he did not want his stepfather to have charge of him. Angus had often made his mother weep. James would not forget it.

"My heart will go with you, my lord, if you depart," said the Queen plaintively. Albany bowed, acknowledging the compliment; but said no more. They left presently, the mother and son; and Albany gazed into the fire and saw his wife's face. To return to her and fair France, where draughts did not blow down passages and where folk were not suddenly murdered and their bodies fouled with bog-silt! He must return soon.

It could not be at once. Before he left Her Grace had her portrait painted with him at a table, hand in hand, she wearing a linen coif of the German fashion. But somebody put a serpent in the picture. It was known by not a few that the Queen, in exchange for a pension from the Cardinal, was sending news into England. But she fell ill of the smallpox, which destroyed her beauty: and after that she had less power.

You like well all such matters as this: the Queen here makes preserves with great delight. So Angus wrote to his sister, telling her also of their safe arrival—he did not dwell on its manner—and their reception at the French King's Court. When the bearer rode into Glamis Clang-Causey was absent, so Jonet had the letter to herself. She sat for a long time scanning it, and trying to picture the kind of life her brothers led now; ruffling it, as Angus so loved to do, at the Court of the fox-nosed monarch, rumoured to be a squire of dames. As soon as she might do so she sent a reply; but its contents seemed dull to her.

Would Angus forget her in his new, brilliant life as Scots Ambassador? Was even quiet, jam-making Queen Claude a cause for wonder? Jonet had heard of that Queen and how while her husband amused himself with women about Court, Claude went to church, where she was devout; her mother Anne of Brittany had been the same. Truly it was strange, and often pitiful, the way in which women must endure their lot; Jonet knew that she must be thankful for her own, and yet some matter was lacking in her marriage. She did not know what it was, and said nothing to anyone, even to her mother-in-law of whom she had grown fond.

7

She had found contentment at Glamis as soon as she had the great keys. The place was hers to warm and keep, to polish and dust and maintain. The servants at first were strange, a little, with a different way of speaking from the Lothian women she had helped to order at Tantallon. But as the days passed she learnt to order these. Among them was a wry-necked girl called Kate, who was said to be the priest John Lyon's daughter. Jonet took little heed of her yet; she was too greatly busied with the myriad rooms in the castle, the buttery and dairy and great flagged kitchen, even the armoury where the men kept swords and mail well polished with sand. Looking out one could see the two bridges built by Glamis' redoubtable grandmother, dowager Isobel: and within were the twelve great silver flagons of which he had boasted, standing on the oak sideboard in the hall. The place had a different air from Tantallon; it was less open, keeping its secrets close within its seven ditches, its moat and containing wall.

She took some time to grow accustomed to the cold. It was pervasive, reaching past one's clothing to the flesh beneath; one must never be idle, for moving warmed the blood. They wore thicker gear here than on the Border, and by winter Jonet was glad to put on two pairs of hose, two petticoats, a gown of grey wool. She left herself with no time to remember the green fields about Bonkle, the gulls wheeling over Tantallon, even the busy street in Edinburgh. Her very brother Angus seemed remote, with his new great affairs; she heard from him in France, but the letter said nothing that could not be read by anyone; he and George had been civilly received at Court as the Scots ambassadors. No doubt the Regent had written privily to King François; at any rate, the pair stayed in France. As for the Queen, there was no news and Jonet did not ask. There was baking to be done and brewing, and butter to be made in the dairy from the cows' cream.

Clang-Causey bided quiet, and she saw him at the high table and in their bed at night. He seemed pleased that she was a good housekeeper; once or twice he complimented her on the better food nowadays, and she reflected that her mother had taught her among much else to know properly hung beef and to see it basted. Clang-Causey seldom interrupted her in the midst of her tasks, but when he did she was careful to be courteous to him. She continued to love her lively mother-in-law, who rode over often; my lady Huntly was only waiting for her old second husband to die before marrying for a third time, to Lord Rothes who was busy divorcing his wife. She was full of gossip and Jonet came to know the folk hereabouts before she met them all; but always kept her counsel.

A tower of strength was the man Patrick Charteris, as my lord had said he would be. He would carry out his orders promptly and well, looking one straight between the eyes when answering anything. His presence consoled her for that of William Lyon, who still hung about though Jonet could think of no reason for dismissing him.

She could not forget the reception of Angus' second letter; Glamis had not been present when she received the first. The letter mentioned Her Grace, not with respect. Glamis took and read it, as was his right, and his frown deepened and he turned away. She was disturbed; Angus' rash swaggering angered many, but it was one of the things about him that Jonet loved. "What is the matter?" she asked her husband; whatever it was, she would rather know of it. He lost no time in telling her.

"I care not for the Earl your brother, and that is the plain truth. There is known to be ill commons between

him and the Queen's Grace, for many wrongs since he left
her alone to ride into England."

"That was years ago. Do folk speak of it still? They
must have little else in their minds." She would always
support Angus, even in fear of blows. So far, Clang-
Causey had not beaten her.

"There were swords drawn in the very heart of
Edinburgh for his cause and that of Arran. Such clamour
is not seemly."

She almost laughed; he made enough clamour himself.
Had he been present at Cleanse the Causeway fight he
would have been the first to draw steel. But he had
turned to face her and his expression was like thunder. "I
am the Queen's man," he said, "and remember it when ye
write or have aught to do with Angus, or any Douglas."

"My lord, he is my brother." The thought of being
separated in all ways from Angus chilled her; she had
hoped that when he and George returned, as they must
some day do, they would ride here often. Now there was
to be no welcome. Her face fell and he was quick to note
it.

"Are ye not blithe here, then, Jonet?" He seemed suddenly like a small boy who is faced with some new
matter; for such reasons she could not hate him. "I love
the life here," she said, and hoped that would satisfy him.
She could never say she loved my lord Glamis himself,
and was glad he did not ask.

Kate Lyon was indeed priest John's daughter, but he had
never sinned in that way again. Her mother had tight-
laced herself to hide the pregnancy, and so Kate was born
with a wry neck and one eye smaller than the other. It
seemed worse to her than it did to other folk, and over the
years she had grown silent and secretive. She had gone
into service at the castle when she was twelve, and did
her duty as it was taught to her; at present she was
polishing the furniture with beeswax, and this brought

her into my lady's chamber. She took the wax and her cloth, and polished the great clothes-chest, making the dark wood shine. Curiosity was too much for her, and she opened the chest; here were my lady's gowns that she had brought with her from her wedding, and her shifts and night-gear.

Kate loved my lady. She seemed always gently spoken, and so beautiful; different from oneself as could be. The gowns were in all colours, blue and scarlet and the colour of cream; one had silver thread through it, and Kate could not resist bringing it out, with its hushing sound and sweet smell of lavender, and putting it against her own ungainly body. It was unlike anything she had ever known; dimly she glimpsed what it must be like to be high-born, and rich, and beautiful. There was a Spanish mirror in the room, and she took the gown to see with her body behind it. There was her face, her wry ugly face, and beauty of the fair stuff beneath. She felt tears rise; she could never be so. She went to put the gown back where it had been, hoping she could fold it as had been formerly done; and turned, and beheld my lady, watching her from the door. Her clear green eyes were empty of anger.

Kate did not wait for Jonet to speak. "My lady, I am sorry. I wanted . . . I wanted . . . to see . . ." Her mouth fell open and the tears coursed down her cheeks. She would be dismissed, whipped, terrible punishment would follow. But Lady Glamis was not angry; how could that be?

"If ye wanted to see the gowns, Kate, I will have ye for my waiting-woman. Can ye kaim hair?"

She was smiling. She had already remarked this poor girl, and knew that if she could win her she would be a faithful servant, like Patrick Charteris. Kate had fallen on her knees. "My lady, my lady, such is too good for me . . . my lord will be angered." She had often enough heard the anger of Clang-Causey, shouting down the stairs and through the castle; how could my lady endure it so gracefully? "My lord will not be angered with yourself,

Kate; and I will tell him it is my wish that ye should serve me," she said.

Kate served her faithfully and well, and grew to love her more and more. By the end Jonet trusted her more than any of her servants except Charteris. They were to see many summers out together.

8

Glamis had its store of legends and ghosts, but only once did Jonet encounter any. She was lying alone in her chamber of a winter's night, Clang-Causey being away in Forfar. Outside the wind was quiet, and the long snows cast their pallid light within the room to the fire's flickering. Kate slept on a pallet beyond the door. There was no warning, no strangeness felt; but in the room there became visible a very tall old man, in a long robe such as men had worn in the time of Bell-the-Cat her grandfather. His long beard brushed her face as if with ice and she knew an instant's fear. But the fire could be seen through him and she knew he was not made of flesh. She lay with open eyes and stared at him. Suddenly, he spoke.

"I was in chains afore ye were born, Jonet Douglas, lang, lang in prison."

Then the shadows claimed him and he was gone. For some reason she did not speak of it to her husband when he returned. No doubt he would know of the legend, but the old man had suffered cruelly and Jonet did not want to expose his memory to scoffing.

In any event she had other matters on her mind; she was with child, and glad of it. The ghostly man never appeared again, nor did Jonet ever find out why he had come and who he might have been. The changes in her body occupied her for the ensuing months, with Clang-Causey oddly gentle; in time the pains started, and Jonet gave birth, easily, to a boy, the heir of Glamis.

"Ye have done well," said Clang-Causey, delight on his face. In some manner the child's arrival justified him to himself; he was no longer the unsuccessful younger brother, the bereaved son. He remained easy to anger, noisy, and mocking; but he treated his wife with deference now that she was the mother of his son.

As for William Lyon, he rode off to some place of his own, and did not return till long after Jonet was up and about again. She hardly noticed his absence except that it brought relief; she watched Johnny Lyon smile and learn to talk, and took great joy of him.

9

"My lord of Albany? He is gone back to France and good riddance. May we never behold his Frenchman's face again."

"He says that he is coming back," said the Queen.

My lord of Arran's eyes roved in his dissipated countenance to rest on Her Grace, seated in a chair by him. She was, he decided, getting stout; but still a fair armful of flesh despite the smallpox. She had striven to win Albany to her bed and no doubt that was one reason why she took it for granted he would return. Margaret Tudor put no low value on her own charms.

And himself? he weighed his assets in the balance, beginning from the days long ago when he and James IV had been cousins and boys together, playing at Stirling in the shadow of the King's unhappy father, watching the great buildings rise that had been chartered from James III's architect favourite, Cochrane, whom with the rest old Bell-the-Cat later hanged over Lauder brig. Later still he, Arran, had taken for his mistress the sister of the King's love, Beatrix Drummond. He and Beatrix did not deal together nowadays although she had borne him children out of wedlock. And later still he—

"Meantime," the Queen broke in, "you and I, my lord, have the power."

"In trust for Your Grace's son the King," put in Arran unctuously. It went without saying that whoever held the person of the King had power. He cast about in his mind for ways to wield it; he was not strong as regarded notions, though most folk had forgotten by now that he had ruined the Scots navy the year of Flodden.

He possessed himself of Her Grace's hand, and kissed

the plump white flesh in lingering fashion. What a fool Angus had been to allow himself to be spirited away from France, leaving his wife to other men! Margaret Tudor needed a man constantly about her; and it was not so ill a task with the reward it brought of having one's will in everything concerning the government. There was plenty of time; the King was young enough.

But Arran should have taken heed to the regency. Ruling jointly with the Queen, as Albany had perforce left him to do, he satisfied nobody. A concourse of noblemen met and decided to recall the Queen's husband Angus from France. Of all evils Angus seemed the least; and his powerful Douglas clan might keep law and order, which was breaking down under Arran.

Angus got word and set sail, George at his elbow. He was glad to be rid of the Court of France and its suave, cynical King who promised everything and did nothing. Also, it was embarrassing to meet Albany, the man who had planned his kidnapping; it made him feel a fool.

They landed, not in Scotland but in England; and rode straight to King Henry's Court.

10

The King of Scots was alone in the room, playing with a dagger my lord Lennox had lately given him. My lord knew how to talk to boys. But he was not here today with his large cheerful presence, and the papingo was dead. Tears rose in James's eyes as they always did when he thought of her; he had never been lonely while she was on his wrist, talking like a human, making him laugh with the words he himself had taught her. She had flown free one day and had been found pecked to death by the wild birds on the Abbey Craig by Stirling. Now he was at Holyrood, but he still thought of the papingo. Birds must be like folk, angry with anyone who was different. That he himself was so he knew already. He was the King; and his tutors Davy Lindsay and Gavin Dunbar said he was doing well. He even knew a little astronomy. But today he had no heart for that and had wanted to be left alone.

It was useless. His mother came in, on the arm of James's master carver, Harry Stuart. Harry was always in her company now and James did not dislike him, handsome and good-natured as he seemed. News had come that the Queen's husband Angus—James could hardly remember him—had left France for England, where he was in high favour with one's uncle Henry VIII. A report had come lately which dwelt on the Earl's height and noble bearing in London. But the Queen did not want him back. So much James knew; he had not yet heard that Margaret was attempting divorce proceedings, and had even offered Angus her Ettrick rents if he would agree. As he had appropriated them from the beginning, this meant nothing.

The Queen kissed her son. "How fares Your Grace

today? I am glad to see ye with a dagger. Every young man should have one, do you not think so, my Harry?"

"Assuredly," replied Harry Stuart, his eyes lazily assessing the situation. He had only to please this ageing, stoutening woman in all ways to better himself. It was easy enough; Her Grace could trust him not to turn his coat, as some had. He looked at the King. The boy was well grown and it was best to make a friend of him. Harry saw the flush which had spread over the pale, oval face at mention of manhood. "The tutors use him like a child," said the Queen aloud. "At his age my brother in England could tilt a lance and run at the ring." She was plaintive; there had been hard words lately in some of her brother's letters, but how could she deal anywhere without money? God knew where it went; her affairs were muddled, not through her own fault. In some way the Queen contrived to blame Angus; the trouble had all started there; if only she were rid of him! But, sooner or later, he would cross the Border from England, and one must be ready to oppose him.

The King was still flushed. "Madam, I too can tilt a lance, on Leith sands." He fell silent. His mother was always plaguing him about the tutors, as though she resented his learning anything. And he liked reading Davy's verse and hearing his talk. But if his uncle of England had run and tilted at his age, it was necessary to do the same. His uncle was his ideal, to be copied in everything; so musical, so learned, so strong and excelling in manly exercises! He himself must spend more time at those. Davy Lindsay might prate if he would, and he, the King, would not listen.

By degrees the Queen succeeded in ridding young James of his tutors, and his education stopped. However, there were compensations. Angus had not yet crossed the Border, and Henry VIII sent young James a sword and a coat of cloth of gold. The coat fitted perfectly. James liked to swagger in it and to wear the sword.

Jonet had word again from her brother; but this time concealed the letter. Clang-Causey was making much clamour about how he himself was the Queen's man, against all Douglases. Jonet did not know what Angus would do, but there was no doubt that he would try to reach the person of the King. It was only a few days before Clang-Causey strode in, scowling.

"Your well-beloved brother, my lady, has disturbed the country's peace as I kent he would if he were permitted to ride home."

She was calm. "In what way?" she asked evenly. His scowl deepened.

"The way will mean nothing to a woman. He scaled the walls of Edinburgh with ladders, and caused Her Grace and the King to take safety in the Castle. They rode up by night to the light of torches, after Her Grace had had the small cannon fired from Holyrood."

"Into the town?" God knew what harm had been done; but she had a vivid picture in her mind of the torchlight procession, the Queen stout and set, her son's red hair flaming, the folk pressing, and Angus; where was he? She dared to ask her husband, who spread out his hands.

"What is it to me, or to any, where Angus is?" he asked roughly.

"I would know that he is safe."

"Very well, I will send Patrick Charteris down." He always ended by deferring to her, though such an idea would itself have made him angry. Charteris returned with the news that Angus had after all retreated to Tantallon. Few folk had been hurt by Her Grace's cannonade, only two priests, two seamen and an old woman. But that was bad enough.

At any rate my brother will be safe in his own place from any force Her Grace can muster at present, Jonet thought. Angus had the valuable support of the King of England,

and the strength of his own Douglas men.

The Queen herself was by now again with Arran, who had raised an army of his own on the excuse that the King was to have been guarded by a rota of lords as arranged, but Angus' presence threatened. Arran had also promised the Queen that he would rid her of her husband. They rode through mud and bramble-thickets to Linlithgow, and all through the night there were comings and goings, whispering and sudden rough raised voices. The Queen lay awake, and Arran, still in his half-armour, heard the clink of gold above the talk; they bribed him without difficulty. Next day he and the Queen took horse again, leaving the armed men mostly behind, keeping only a small number for guard on the road.

"What are they at?" asked the Queen of the army. "Why do they not ride with us?"

Arran gave her some evasive answer; he would not tell her the truth yet, or she might well turn her horse's head and harangue the men into some show of obedience. He admitted her courage; but it should not stand in his way. The bribe had been handsome enough.

They rode on. At last out of the winter dark there loomed a half-finished building. "Where in the world are we?" asked the Queen, and again, "What has become of the men?"

Then he told her. They were at his palace of Hamilton, which was still building. "Ye may rest here," he said, "there are comforts here."

"But why did we not rest at Linlithgow?" She was suspicious; Arran let his glance fall. "Angus may get the King's person," he told her. "It is unsafe to make war on him, accordingly. We must bide our time."

"Traitor!" screamed the Queen. But there was nothing she could do. Not for the first time, she was a lone woman surrounded by men she could not trust. It was one of the reasons why she had married Angus, years ago: loneli-

ness. She began to weep, then dried her tears. Tears would
not change anything; she knew as much by now. If only
there were a man she could trust, could love! But such was
not Arran, any more than her husband, or Cardinal Wolsey.

The months passed. Arran himself sat back to watch
events. Others put themselves in touch with him,
uncertain of what would happen. When the time was ripe,
they would fight someone somewhere. But privately
Arran knew that he would fight on the side of Angus. It
was only politic, taking thought for the future.

Clang-Causey had acquired a rare goshawk, and rode out
with it on his wrist beyond Glamis in the early day. The
turf was still pallid with frost, and he let the bird fly free,
admiring its barred wings and white, black-striped belly
as it fluttered and swooped in flight. It reminded him of
something; he searched in his mind, and found his wife
there: like the hawk, with her proud graceful movements
and bright eye. Yet he might own the hawk, but never
Jonet. The knowledge tore at him. She was courteous at
bed and board, never denied him his rights, had borne him
a son, and yet . . . *Jonet, Jonet woman, I havena ye!* He felt
his soul's cry.

He had watched her, day and night; a woman who lived
with him, day in and day out, yet never wearied him, for he
could not reach her. Was her secret contained in her proud
Douglas blood? The Douglases were almost kings in the
land now. Yet if she had shown such pride he would have
struck her, and it had never happened. She was always
gentle and subservient to him, yet he did not possess her,
and knew it. He could kneel at her feet, and it would be no
different; and, of course, he would never so kneel. The
whole matter plagued him and he did not see what more he
could do. He would ride back and see Jonet now, whatever
she was at. He liked to come on her thus and surprise her,
hoping perhaps to take her secret by assault.

The wild bird swooped and then returned, its beak full. Clang-Causey made his horse canter back, the goshawk perched again on his wrist. It had been well trained in Germany.

Jonet was in the solar with her son, young John, and Lady Huntly her mother-in-law, the latter discontented because her old husband still lived and Lord Rothes, to whom she had an eye, would soon look elsewhere. Old Huntly was downstairs and had slept in the dais-chamber; his legs no longer supported the climb. They had stayed overnight at Glamis and would return home tomorrow. It was a long journey for the old Lieutenant.

Jonet had risen especially early. A neighbour, the Laird of Pitcur's wife, had gone with her husband and Aunt Marjory Ochterlony lately to Edinburgh, and had brought back a fairing of orange-apples. They made good preserve, peel and all, and, before they should spoil, Jonet had got herself and Kate and the other women into aprons to prepare the fruit and expensive sugar and put the mixture on to boil. Her hands seemed still sticky with the juice despite having rinsed them. Johnny had come to watch the proceeding and to have his taste of the syrup.

She watched him confidently; he had learned to walk and was healthy. His father had been pleased at his birth and so had she, although a second pregnancy had already started and she could have wished it a little less soon. But life was pleasant; she could ride out to the Market Muir among the booths and to St Fergus' Fair in November, and talk with her neighbours who came there from all parts, and who were her friends nowadays and, accordingly, Clang-Causey's; there were fewer feuds at Glamis since she had come as a bride.

Clang-Causey himself stood talking now to old Huntly, his stepfather, who sat by the fire drinking wine; and the handsome silent grandson he had brought, his son's son, standing behind his chair. Huntly had commanded the left wing at Flodden and still talked of it, though the years had passed.

"I mind your good lady's brother Angus was by me as we rode away, and left half Scotland dead on the field," he said. "Dark as night it was, that September day: and all the King's fine brass cannon from France firing in the air, for they were set too high. But the master gunner was killed at the outset, and no man kenned what to do in the storm that came."

He sipped his wine. Clang-Causey listened in some impatience. He himself had, when all was said, lost three uncles at Flodden and had little time for old men's stories. He almost interrupted Huntly as he talked. "Get my lady down to the hall," he commanded one of the servants. As it often did, a desire had come over him to see Jonet; merely to let his eyes rest on her was pleasant, tormenting, strange.

The servant went up and presently Jonet herself came downstairs, leading Johnny by the hand; at sight of his father the child shrank back against his mother's skirts. 'Come, quickly; do not dally," said Clang-Causey impatiently. The time would go slowly enough till his son was a man; he must learn to ride and shoot, and use a sword as soon as he could hold it. It was of no use to let him cling to his mother. At the same time he knew pride in the sturdy little boy and the slight thickening of Jonet's body above her kirtle. Two boys would be better than one, remembering what had happened in his own youth. If this second child were a son he would call him George after his dead brother.

Huntly had risen, leaning on his staff. "How fares my lady this day?" he asked in his old voice, admiring the sight of the bonnie woman whom everyone from Forfar to Inverness loved. She wore a stuff kirtle today for the jam-making, but it would have been the same had she been clad in silk; her beauty made one forget whatever she was wearing. And, unlike many fair women, she had a low sweet voice. God had bestowed much on her, thought the old Lieutenant.

He turned to his grandson, bringing him forward. "They say he is like his mother's dam, the dead King's love, Margaret Drummond," he told them, with the swift changing of one thought for another of the old. "He has grown tall since last ye saw him."

The tall boy blushed, and Jonet smiled at him, thinking that she might indeed be looking on the fair face of the late King's love, so handsome was he. Old Huntly was still talking. "They say the King took Janet Kennedy for her body, and Margaret Drummond for her soul, and both bore him bastards." The yellowed teeth showed in a grin. "Why, the two of them—the King and Meg—would sit together on the banks of Tay, watching the river run past, in a great silence. The King wrote a poem till her there."

"If she was silent she was a fine woman," said Clang-Causey, and laughed loudly at his own pleasantry. But Huntly had forgotten him. "She is laid in earth at Dunblane," he said, "and soon I will be also. I mind they said old King Henry of England had a hand in her death, so soon before the English marriage."

"It will never be known," said Jonet, taking Johnny on her lap. "My mother, their sister, used to speak of it sometimes; all three of them, Margaret and Eupham and Sybilla, died in great pain, it was thought of poisoned mushrooms."

"That could happen to anyone," said Clang-Causey. "They aye bring a clamour of poison at a sudden death."

Jonet shivered a little, as though someone walked over her grave. Then she made herself smile on, listening to the men, and Kate came to take Johnny from her and go back with him upstairs, and my lady Huntly joined them, and what they had been saying was already forgotten by the company. But Jonet remembered.

Before he rode off—he would not use a litter—Huntly the Lieutenant had a word with her alone.

"Ye have done well," he said, "in healing quarrels. But make no fast friends with the Forbeses. Deceit is in their hearts, as well as lust. I ken what I say; none of my blood will bide under the same roof with one of them." It was an old blood-feud whose origins had been forgotten, and when a Forbes met a Huntly, to this day, they fought one another. But Jonet maintained her silence concerning it; Lord Huntly was her friend, and my lord Forbes also.

As for Clang-Causey, he railed at the old man's talk after they had gone. "All that about folk who are dead, what boots it now?" he said, scowling. His mother had married Huntly while he was still a boy, and thereafter had neglected her Glamis sons altogether. Perhaps her lack had made John Lyon what he was; perhaps not. But he was proud of his wife and the way she handled difficult folk. Not only the Forbeses had given way to Jonet's charm, but even the Ogilvys; and he had allowed it, surprising himself; Ogilvy had when all was said killed his father. Now Elinor Ogilvy and Jonet exchanged embroidery-patterns. Let the dead bury their dead, after all; she had taught Clang-Causey as much as that.

There was a fierce storm that autumn, which tore off the thatch from the cottages and left it spinning on the roads, while the banked fires were whipped into flame and caused great danger. In Edinburgh the roof flew off David's Tower and the folk blamed the Queen for ill luck, especially as there had been skirmishes on the Borders and the English had set fire to the Regent Albany's lately rebuilt Abbey of Jedburgh. But all had not gone well for them; they were surprised overnight by what they thought was a Scots force, but it was only their own horses stampeding at sight of the flames; they shot at them with bows and arrows before they could see them, and many were injured or destroyed by the fire, and twenty plunged over a cliff. Nothing of the kind had been known since the dark times before James IV, and folk again murmured against the

English Queen. News filtered north; the Earl of Angus had
at last confronted Her Grace, with her son, at the Castle, to
which they had fled before Angus' outrage over the walls of
Edinburgh. But the two parties were rumoured to be on
friendly terms in discussing their divorce. Later, Parlia-
ment was opened by the King and his mother, with Angus
bearing the crown before them and Arran the sword.
Everything promised peace.

But Jonet was not at ease. There had been few letters
from her brother, and she even wondered if Clang-Causey
had kept them from her. She had given birth to George,
her second son, some days since, and knelt in the chapel
telling her beads, while John the priest recited his offices
and the candles swayed in the wind. The man William
Lyon knelt a few paces behind: she did not turn her head.
Now as on many occasions she felt cut off from her family,
her mother, Alison and Margaret and Elizabeth and the
rest. They had not been to visit her because of Clang-
Causey's ban against the Douglases. Perhaps now he will
admit my brother to be on the way to power, she thought;
having met the King face to face, Angus could scarcely be
called fugitive. But he abode still at Tantallon. She knew
that he would not be anxious for the divorce from the
Queen, as it would harm their young daughter Madge. Her
Grace seemed to have no remembrance of the girl, and
never sought her out or mentioned her.

Clang-Causey was away, in Elgin on business; she did
not know when to expect him back as he had sent no word.
She was surprised to see the azure lion banner suddenly
against the dark day; the storm had been followed by
frosts, and now it was January, the bitter time; she wore
thick gear like the rest. Her husband was handing down a
woman from the saddle, bundled into grey shawls and
warm clothing. She went out, and saw him lout over the
woman's hand. The Queen! What was she about, so far
north?

Jonet stayed where she was, and made her curtsy as Her

Grace came up on the arm of Glamis. To her surprise, the
stout woman, one of whose eyes was filmed over now, fell
upon her kissing her, mouthing sundry things. "I came to
you . . . you had gentle hands last time . . . spare me a bed, I
pray, for I have ridden far . . ."

Shock came to Jonet: as before, the Queen was in labour;
her short breaths showed it, and she began to cry out a
little with the pains. Jonet hurried her upstairs to her own
chamber, undressed her with the help of Kate and laid her
in her shift on the bed. The straining had already begun; in
the intervals of it the narrow unequal eyes sought hers.
She stayed by the Queen's side with a warm caudle for
comfort. The hours passed. She had asked nothing. Surely
this could not have come about from the meeting of the
Queen and Angus again? They were said to be on ill terms,
despite the public show. As though she had spoken aloud,
the querulous voice came.

"It is . . . not your brother's child. It is Harry Stewart's.
Tell no one." The pock-marks showed livid from
Margaret's straining, and a trickle of saliva came from her
mouth. Jonet wiped it away with a cloth. "Have no fear,
Your Grace," she heard herself saying. "Have no fear; ye
are safe at Glamis."

"Ye . . . are *his* sister. It must seem . . . strange . . . but I
trust . . .

A loud cry came and the child was born, and lived. Jonet
handed it to Kate to have its mouth and nostrils cleaned.
The fire in the room blazed cheerfully. She made the sick
woman as comfortable as she could and when night came,
slept on a pallet by her. Clang-Causey had not come near,
and had said nothing to her; he had not forbidden her to
write to her brother, and as soon as she could be alone she
did so.

My brother, I commend me heartily to ye. The Queen is
here for the time. I pray ye have mercy on her. She is a
woman, and ill.

There could be no harm in that; she had betrayed no one.

No word came in reply from Angus, and by then Her Grace had ridden off to raise an army: the child was put to nurse and would be sent, later, wherever it might. The Queen had murmured of Perthshire, and that was not so far. Glamis rode by her. "I am the Queen's man," he said, as he had said it many times before. "I will do Her Grace service as I may."

He would meet Angus soon, in battle at Linlithgow, in the presence of the King.

The King was angry, with a cold anger which increased, like ice freezing. They had come into his presence, the two Douglases, Angus and George, and with them their old uncle Kilspindie who they knew would divert him with sword-play and the like, for Kilspindie was a strong old ruffian and could hold his own in everything but wit. They had sat down in his presence, the pair of them, with their hats on; and had told him, James, he was in their charge and that without their word, nothing could be done in Scotland. They were boasting, naturally; they had no control over the shifty Borderers or the fierce Highlanders further north. But they had the King's person, and that was worth much.

'Where is my mother?'" said the King, and George Douglas laughed.

"Your Grace's mother holds not to her liege lord. Where she may be we know not. It is no great matter."

The King flushed scarlet, then white, and turned away. He must thole them, for now, he knew; the courtyard was full of their men. But soon, as soon as it might be done, he would win free. The time could be spent in thinking of ways. Harry Stewart, his mother's lover, would aid him, if he could get word to him. Harry would get arms for him into some secure place. It must all be kept secret, so secret that not a man knew except themselves. Then when he might, he, the King, would win free.

His first attempt was disastrous. The porter would not open the castle gate, and James drew his dagger on the poor devil, stabbed him and saw him fall. There was trouble with my lord of Angus after that; James' dagger, Lennox' gift, was taken away. His mother had said his tutors treated him as a child, but he would be glad now of the sight of Gavin Dunbar and kind Davy. But they had gone, with everyone; and there was only old Kilspindie for diversion. James tilted at arms with him, had mock fights with him, and called him Greysteel from a character in a poem. But there was no time for poetry now.

Quite suddenly word came to him from his mother, borne by a messenger who outwitted the Douglases. She had raised six hundred men in the north and was marching home; could James reach Linlithgow?

"I would visit my mother." He always made his statements to the brothers short and curt, and they had no knowledge of the fire that burned inside him. Angus shrugged, assuming that in their charge as he would be, the Queen could do little harm. They took horse and rode towards Linlithgow Palace, where once James IV had walked with Margaret Drummond beneath the cherry trees, which by now for lack of care gave only thin sour fruit. It was autumn, and the King's hair echoed the blaze of colour the trees made, with the wind making a few dead leaves already whirl along the paths. The Douglas guards jingled behind him.

It was not long till they saw armed men. George Douglas drew closer to the King in his saddle, and jerked his own head at his brother. The whelp had outwitted them! It was necessary to keep a cool head. There might not be so many.

Angus was smiling. He had known well enough about the Queen's army, and had distributed silver to good purpose. Arran was with her, and Arran would lead the men over. As for Lennox, he must take what came.

The armies were spread out on the plain. One one side rode the Queen, with Harry Stewart, his brothers, and the assorted army she had gathered in the north. On the other was the slim red-haired boy, tall already, seated between the two Douglases. A roar went up at sight of the King; and the men shoved forward together, going across to him like a great wave, most of them; others began to fight under Lennox, as they had promised Her Grace. But the numbers by now were far and away unequal, and soon the fighting died. Cries of "A Douglas! A Douglas!" still sounded about the bull's head banner nearby the Queen. Lennox himself fought valiantly, flaying left and right with his sword. At last he was beaten to his knees, his horse dead under him from a Douglas thrust, its bowels gushing out.

Harry Stewart was wounded; one of his brothers was dead. Lennox rose to his feet and spread out his hands, in sign of surrender. Seeing him the King spurred forward. "Lennox!" he screamed. "Lennox!"

His bridle was caught and his horse jerked round. George Douglas was holding it; his teeth showed in a grin. The King struggled, weeping with rage. "Bide here, my liege," said George. "Were they to get hold of an arm of yours, we would hold ye by the leg; ay, and see ye torn in pieces ere we part with your person."

Hamilton of Finnart, Arran's bastard, approached my lord Lennox, who had given himself up to the King's mercy. The thing was quickly done; a dagger flashed; Lennox dropped to the ground, his blood flowing red, then it stopped; he lay there dead in a pool of it. The King was sobbing and still calling his name.

Later, everyone saw Arran kneel down by the dead

Lennox—he was his uncle, but they had long fallen out over Arran's divorces—and sing his praises in a sickening fashion. Back at the rear, the Queen was weeping. Her army had melted like snow, Harry was hurt, and she was no nearer her son. She rode forward; maybe they would not harm her. She avoided the sight of Lennox lying in his blood, and joined the King's party. James, his face already swollen with weeping, would not at first look at her; but later they greeted one another.

It was evident that the Douglases would not share the guardianship of the King with anyone, least of all the rota of nobles whom Albany had carefully selected, before he went, to govern. Soon Her Grace withdrew to Stirling, where Harry Stewart now was; it was whispered that she had gone through a form of marriage with him, but others denied it, saying she wished to marry Albany, who was now a widower, on his return. As for the King, he kept silence; nobody was allowed access to him. Lennox' two young sons had been taken out of the country, and sent to France.

11

Old Huntly was dead, and Jonet's lively mother-in-law duly married that ladies' man, Lord Rothes; but three years of it killed her. Jonet missed her bright clothes and rattlepated gossip; my lord was already courting a third wife, and had more bastards than anyone in the county.

No visitors, then, came from Huntly; but the Forbeses remained her friends, free of the old enmity between the clans. Lord Forbes was a Highlander, very tall with fiery dark eyes; he had strict notions of his honour, and it was as much as Jonet could do to prevent her husband falling out with him in their very hall. One day my lord rode in with tidings from Edinburgh.

"They say the Queen and her new husband had to kneel for mercy before my lord of Angus himself, who granted it at last. And my lord of Angus—your pardon, my lady—is letting the King know of matters he should not, and doing of them forbye. They say he rolled with a serving-maid into the very midden at the Castle of Stirling, and he is but turned fifteen."

Jonet said nothing, but her mind was troubled. She knew that the King had received no more book-learning, though the Douglases kept him contented with feats of arms through old Kilspindie. But now it seemed that he was being led to fill his mind with women; certainly he had grown to be of an age when he was no longer a child, but . . . Yet she still remained silent, fearful lest Clang-Causey turn the matter to high words. She was under no deceit concerning his hate for the Douglases. Yet their writ ran nowadays through all Scotland, except the Highlands.

"My lord of Albany would be sore displeased if he could see the way things are now," observed Lord Forbes, playing a tattoo with his fingers on his sword-hilt. "They say he canna come to Scotland again because the French King wants war with the Emperor, and has invaded Italy."

Clang-Causey scoffed. "He canna come back because his lady wife is dead, and has left all her money to a kinswoman, so that Albany cannot come with his hands full of gold here, as before."

"He spent the gold well enough for Scotland," said Jonet. Her husband turned a quelling glance on her. "Whisht, woman! I know what I speak of."

"Well, well, the French didna profit from their raids into Italy in the last reign," admitted Forbes. "There will be much inlaid armour and bright swords in use that should maybe have been left hanging on the wall in their castle towers. They brought home the great pox with them last time, and they called it the Italian sickness but other folk call it the French disease. It would be better to bide at home."

He had turned Clang-Causey's anger away from his wife, and presently began to speak of family matters. Jonet turned her head in its round velvet hood towards him. She was always glad to see folk; they reminded her of other things besides the passing of time. She had four children now; the boys, dour Margaret and pretty Elizabeth, named for her mother's sister, growing old enough to crawl, to walk, to ride. Johnny was still being beaten by his father for not managing his pony properly. He was easily cowed; it was a pity. Kindness and patience were better, but her husband would none of them.

Forbes had brought his bastard daughter Annabella with him today. He had called her after a royal ancestress and loved her better than all his children by his wife. She wore a dress with a grand pair of sleeves, embroidered with gold thread and pearls. Little Elizabeth wandered from her mother's side and went to stroke the pearls, the light shining on her curly, flaxen hair.

"My mother has grand sleeves forbye," she said. Everyone laughed. My lord Forbes put his arm about Elizabeth, who was already a little flirt, and gazed up at him.

"This is a bonnie wee lass," he said. "I have a son at home would make a match till her."

"She is young yet," said Jonet. Clang-Causey frowned a little; any arrangements of the kind should be left to him. But an alliance with the Forbes clan, despite the never-ending feud with the Huntlys, would be welcome enough. "In time, in time," he said, and my lord nodded approval. "May there be time for all things," he said. "They tell me Her Grace's new husband Harry Stewart of Avandale has children by another wife. I fear Her Grace is a laughing-stock. It is pity of her, for the good she could have done at first. Now nobody thinks her aught."

The talk went on and the wine-cups round, and Jonet thought of Angus, who wrote often but had not managed to ride north to visit her, so beset was he, and would hardly let the young King out of his sight, even to go and embrace his own daughter, young Madge Douglas, who they said was grown most haughty at Tantallon. As for George, he had been twice to Pittendriech but had not come on to Glamis; he had taken to the new religion which was creeping in from England; it suited his rough plain ways. King Henry VIII was said to disapprove of it, but it was by no means certain what that monarch believed now; he had cast off his Queen and had a woman named Anne Bullen about him. Perhaps he and his sister were more like one another than it had seemed at first, although Henry still objected strongly to the Queen of Scots' divorce, and Angus said nothing of it for fear it would harm his daughter. What a coil things were in, and all for folks' liking!

She brought her mind back to listen to Lord Forbes again. His dark eyes regarded her; he thought of her as a comely woman, such as he could have loved had she been free of her husband. "Ye should take Jonet to Court," he was saying, "to see the King and her brother. She has served ye many a year in the north."

"What is there to see?" said Clang-Causey. "Her Grace is ta'en up with her new man, and the King is under governance of my lady's brother."

"Then let her see her brother; and there will be dancing, and cards and the like, now the King is near manhood."

Clang-Causey answered nothing. But afterwards he said, "Ye heard my lord concerning it. Would ye like to go?"

Longing arose in her; to see town once more, away for a while from the north with its cold and the constant household round! Yet she had friends here too.

He was watching her. "Well, speak."

"If it is your wish, I would like it."

"Then get together your grand gear, and we will go."

Pleasure and surprise filled her mind; he did not as a rule ask her what she wanted, and she had not thought he would accede to my lord's suggestion, if only because it had been made by another.

12

They stopped again at Innerpeffray on their way south. Over the years the Drummonds had scattered; the legend was still told about how the old lord, long dead, had struck a herald for murmuring against the Angus marriage. John of Innerpeffray himself was now an old man; he liked to talk of books, and Clang-Causey was of no good to him. His only son, the second John, had married the daughter of James IV and Margaret Drummond after her first husband, young Huntly, had died abroad. She was a quiet woman of perhaps thirty, not showing a trace of the passion that must have conceived her. She had borne her second husband a large number of daughters, and with their births and care hardly ever left Innerpeffray.

"We will take a house in the Canongate," boasted Glamis of the Edinburgh visit. Jonet laid a hand on his arm. "That will be expensive, if indeed it is to be had," she said. "Let us take one a little way out of town, to be free of the smoke." Her mind ran back to the children, left behind in the clear Forfar air. They were safe enough with their nurses and tutor, and Patrick Charteris had been put in charge of the estate.

"Ye are a good wife enough," Clang-Causey, looking at her. The compliment pleased her; they did not come often, and meant more from him than from another.

They took a house at Leith to be near the Court for Easter. It was Lent still and everyone ate fish, but how different here from the dry, dreary stockfish year after year at Glamis! She was used to have it sweetened with lavender, but here there was no need, and no penance. The fishwives brought their wares fresh caught every morning, in baskets balanced on their heads. The harsh east-coast cries they made were welcome, for it was not only herring they sold but haddock and cod and mullet and salmon, the last very cheap. The good food and sea-breezes cheered Jonet and she was glad they had come; once or twice they glimpsed the King tilting on Leith sands. She began to wish that they had brought the children, for Johnny at least would have liked to see the sea, and the sights of the capital.

But Court waited. They rode up the slope to where lights shone from the Castle, for dark came early still. The bulk of David's Tower, with its battlements mended, jutted again to the stars.

Clang-Causey was gloomy. He had begun to regret coming. He had no small talk, and he was jealous of his wife's anxiety to see her brother. But Jonet was happy, knowing she looked her best in a gown of new scarlet, and pearls sewn in her coif. Glamis glanced almost shyly at her by the light of their torches: he could still hardly believe in the possession of so much beauty, and her waist still jimp despite having borne four children. Her parted hair gleamed gold beneath the coif in the torchlight. He would be proud to show her to the King, but the lad was said to fancy women already, with Angus' encouragement, and he had best keep his royal hands off the lady of Glamis.

Angus himself came to greet them, with an arm flung about the shoulders of a red-haired boy with long pale features and secret eyes. Jonet made her curtsy to the King and privately wondered that Angus should have aged so. There were deep lines carved between nose and mouth, and he had let his beard grow above his ruff.

The King was silent, and Jonet had the notion that he disliked the possessive arm. She tried to talk to him, but found him cold and sullen. He hardly looked at Clang-Causey, very fine that night in velvet, but his eyes raked

Jonet.

"Now we will have some dancing," Angus said, as though it were a treat for a child. He is one no longer, Jonet thought, and you should know it. Beyond, some fiddlers struck up, and the crowd began to separate into dancers and watchers.

"Will ye lead out with me, my lady Glamis?" asked the King. Jonet disliked the sweaty cold of his fingers' touch, and protested that she was no longer young.

"Why, ye might be eighteen," said Angus heartily.

James led her out, accordingly, and she found that she remembered the steps well enough. Glamis and Angus did not dance but remained in talk, she knew not about what.

Presently her brother George joined them. Her impulse was to leave the dancing and run to him, but she must not discountenance the King.

George looked even older than Angus: his hair was grey. It was as though she had been in a hundred years' sleep at Glamis: it seemed suddenly very far off.

The King danced well, in his plain tunic and his hat, which he kept on his head, bearing a heron's plume and the great balas ruby his father, James IV, had worn at the time of his wedding. When the music quickened to make a galliard he laughed and to her disgust Jonet felt his hand fondle her breast through the scarlet gown.

"Ye are a lovesome woman . . . for a Douglas."

She drew back from him. "Your Grace, such actions are not seemly. They are shameful. And the Douglases have kept your land at rest these many years."

She saw the hatred grow in his eyes. He did not ask her to dance again, and later, while she was in talk with Angus and George, watched him lead out a strange dark girl with thick mannish eyebrows, whom she had already noted. Her name was Margaret Erskine, and she was newly the wife of Sir James Douglas of Lochleven, kin of Jonet's own. James V seemed to favour Douglas women.

The fiddles sounded high in the chamber, and the crowd was brightly clad, moving like coloured fragments of emerald, ruby, rose, and the gleam of gold.

But she could see Glamis standing with a restless expression on his face, and knowing he would not have been diverted by the talk with her brothers, she got herself ready to leave.

They rode back past the Nor' Loch with its brooding water in the dark, and past the little chapel at its south end. They reached the house at last and found a torch left burning in the staple to light them in. But Glamis seemed strangely flushed, and would say little.

"Are ye well?" she asked, troubled. His health was generally good, but tonight he was unlike himself.

"I have an ache in my guts," he said coarsely. "Like enough it was with hearkening to Douglas talk this night." He spat into the fire. "The King likes not your brothers," he said. "Angus should have a care what he is at. Her Grace does not show herself; she is with her new man in Perthshire. What is all of it to us? I would we were home."

She thanked God Clang-Causey had not seen the King's behaviour with her: there would have been swords out.

"Go to bed," she said, "it is late, and by morning you will feel better, or I will put a herb-poultice on."

But during the night she heard him groan, and by the morning his face was grey. He turned his head away from his breakfast, and would not leave his bed.

"I will send for a physician," she said anxiously. That personage came, and after their manner did little good. He blooded Glamis, who seemed the weaker for it.

His eyes were closed. He was still in pain, not sharp but dull. She felt his belly with gentle fingers: it was taut. He began to murmur like a man in delirium, but he knew her.

"Jonet, woman, I think that I am like to die."

"Never that," she said, and tried to devise ways of easing

him, but could not. She felt forsaken in a strange land. If Glamis were to die what would become of her here? Angus would not spare the time from his great affairs to take heed of her. Glamis would have been taken ill at home, but for herself and her craving to see the Court. And it had been worth little, except that she had seen Angus and George again. Now the physician had made matters worse than ever, in a rich city where one paid, and paid. She would not send for another.

In any case there was no need. Towards the evening Glamis gave a great cry, and thereafter sank into stupor. Jonet sent not for a physician, but for a priest. Glamis was dead by the time he came, and received the Sacrament on his cold tongue, in case there was a part of him which still felt, still listened. But he was dead, and she was left alone. It came to her that she had been fond enough of Clang-Causey. There could have been a worse husband.

Angus rode down to console her and to aid her in arranging the journey of the body back to Glamis. They came and brought cerements, and put the spiced bowels in a closed jar. When all was ready she rode off, no longer in scarlet, by the coffin. It was a long way, and Angus had offered her the King's guards to protect her on the journey. Why did he keep so many guards about the King? The people would not harm him, and his mother was elsewhere. The thought of their fear was more real now than her sorrow. She was growing used to that and to being a widow. Mourning her dead she rode back north, and the neighbours, for his widow's sake, watched in wake for Clang-Causey, whom they had never loved.

13

Jonet had heard Mass in Glamis chapel and had stayed on after the others went. The old priest, John Lyon, Kate's father, who had been with them since before she came as a bride, was douting the candles and a thin trail of blue, acrid smoke rose in the still air. A little way behind, again watching her as always, William Lyon knelt. His presence disturbed her prayers. She could not fault him: there was no reason why he should not remain in the chapel if he wished, and yet she longed for him to be gone from about her.

He did not go, and when she came out into the sunlight he followed her. She was aware of his presence and his familiar, whining voice. At last she turned her head.

"I would be alone," she said, and looked full at him. William's gait cringed in some manner although he held himself straight enough. The pale stare met her own.

"It is not for a fair lady like yourself to be solitary. There are many rough folk in the countryside would do ye harm. It were best to have a man by ye."

"No one will do me harm within thirty miles. Go about your business, and leave me to mine." She was not used to speak so curtly to anyone, and the act spoiled the late Mass for her. She should show forbearance to this creature; after all, God had made them both.

A sudden longing to ride south to Tantallon came to her. She could not rid herself of it, and yet she had only lately returned to the north with Glamis' body. But the more she thought of it the more she wanted it, and the longing grew so strong that before many days were out she sent for Patrick Charteris and bade him order the packing of her gear. He nodded gravely, and went with few words to carry out his task. Afterwards William sidled up again.

"Yon Patrick takes overmuch upon himself. He does not act as a servant should. One would think him the master here."

He gave a little snicker, and she turned on him.

"Patrick is honest and faithful, and does his duty. I would not be without him. Hold your peace."

"And ye are riding to Tantallon, I heard them say?"

"Listeners hear no good. If I choose to ride to Tantallon it is my concern and no other's."

She had half hoped that continuing in this way would rid her of him; no other man would have endured it. But he was still at her side, pestering her. His next words she heard with disbelief.

"Ye maun ride, lady, because ye have no man; lacking one, ye are without solace. I would comfort ye, in your bed and out; and ye need never leave Glamis."

"Go from me," she said. If her lord had been here that would have been the end of it, but because he was not, she had to endure such talk. None of her own kind would have dared speak so, even now.

"Ye will maybe be sorry, lacking me."

"Go, I said." She rose from where she had been sitting by the great hall fire—the days were still cold—and went to where the children were. Johnny had gained a measure of confidence since his father had died and he had come into the title. There was no one to beat him now. He was diverting himself with a piece of sheep's gut, knotting it and beguiling it into a skein and out again.

"I am going to the south," she said, "to see your uncle."

The children showed dismay.

"But, Mama," said Elizabeth, "it is no time at all since ye were in Edinburgh." Their reproachful eyes were on her and she felt guilt rise.

"I shall not be long away," she said. "I am—restless." Was not that the very thing William Lyon had said? It would be intolerable to think of him as governing her in any way.

The ride south was uneventful, the summer roads dry. She felt the green warmth of the Border country envelop her at last, and spurred east to Tantallon. When she saw it rise, square-set and red, before her, she felt tears of joy and relief come.

"Patrick, is it not a bonnie sight?" she said to the man, who rode by her in silence.

He answered respectfully, as was his wont.

"It is a great stronghold, my lady." And so it was, but home to her. She was received with pleasure by the Douglas women, Isobel and the rest. They led her to where a stately child sat in a blue gown, sewing.

"Madge, it is your good aunt from the north. Put by your work a while."

"She is so diligent," Isobel's voice went on, "that she will never be without a task. See how small and fine her stitches are! One day she will make some nobleman a fine wife."

Young Margaret Douglas had risen and made her curtsy, but looking at the fair remote face and flaxen hair Jonet wondered if such talk were good for her. It must drive her back within herself to be talked of as if she had no hearing, even though she were a queen's daughter.

Later Jonet was able to speak alone with the girl, and asked her, on purpose to make friends, to take her up to the high lookout chamber from where one could watch the sea. It was windy there. The wind ruffled Madge's sedate curls.

"I have missed the sea," said Jonet, "at Glamis, I think more than anything." She stared down at the turbulent waves. How pleasant to stand here, and watch, and not have to sail upon them! One was safe at Tantallon.

They had not heard footsteps behind them, and when the Earl spoke in his deep voice they whirled about, their skirts spinning and caught by the wind.

He laughed with pleasure. "Sister Jonet, how good to see

ye! I did not know ye were with us. It is pure fortune that I came down to see my daughter. What think you of her? Is she not well grown?"

Jonet agreed that Madge was grown, but within herself continued to be troubled about the child. She was treated like a royal princess and deferred to, but maybe the day would come when she would have to be of everyday. Yet there seemed no danger of that. Angus talked with confidence of the King, who had been left in George's charge.

"He is dear to me," said Angus. "He is the son I never had." Madge had gone back to her women by then, and did not hear his words, which she would have resented, for she loved her father and thought herself first with him always.

Jonet heard more about young Madge to trouble her, when she and Angus talked alone. Evidently the child's mother, whom Madge scarcely knew and whose very mention she feared, had tried to bring about a wicked thing. She had offered her daughter in marriage to the brother of the man she was now with, a personage named the Captain of Doune, a rough soldier. Madge had somehow heard of it and kept herself close, but had nightmares.

"Send her to me in the north," begged Jonet. "I will see that she is kept safe." What an unnatural mother the Queen was! Yet her son loved her. Madge herself could be nothing to her half-brother; the King and she had hardly met.

"The time will come when they may be free to do so," said Angus pleasantly, and Jonet wondered if he meant what he said. Perhaps he loved the King too well to part with the boy, or maybe the giving of authority royal, which had happened last year, had been a sham. Jonet feared the paths into which his high place was leading her brother. He had once been a handsome, carefree young man; now he was watchful and careworn. Would it not be better to let the King govern with his councils, and withdraw to Tantallon?

"Ye would be at enough leisure to ride north and visit Glamis," she said. "I would like that well."

"I would like it myself, for my days are full of business, and it would be pleasant to sit by ye, Jonet, and drink your small-ale." But he made no effort to free the King, or to leave himself more leisure.

Jonet returned to the north, stopping for a night at Innerpeffray on the way. Everything was quiet there and there was no news. She had lost the sense of urgency that had made her visit Tantallon, and was glad to be returning to the children and Glamis. When she saw the familiar towers rise beyond their wall she was thankful: this, after all, was her home till her death, and the duties that awaited her there made up her life, and she need trouble none.

14

"Will Your Grace hunt the morn?"

"If the weather holds, no doubt."

The red-haired boy by the window tried to sound nonchalant. The morn: tomorrow. If Angus, his gaoler—he loathed him and all his kin—knew what was in his mind!

He kept his back turned so as to give nothing away, no brightening of the eyes, no pallor of excitement, almost of dread. He, James Stewart, must never seem to be afraid. He gave no sign, and stared out through the new glass windows of his palace of Falkland at the sea of summer green and the far Ochils where, God willing, he would ride in haste tomorrow. If it rained, it would be the next dry day. The plans were laid. With a clear sky, surely fortune would be with him. If the plan failed, they would be more than ever on their guard with him. He had not forgotten George Douglas' insulting words at Linlithgow. Tear him apart sooner than set him free? Well, it was they who would be so torn. He would outlaw them, these Douglases, all of their hated race, every man, woman and child of it. He had vowed it time and again over this past year. Cut them off root and branch . . . was that in Holy Writ? At any rate, that was what he would do.

Root and branch. The summer trees would be in thick leaf and would hide him tomorrow. He would outdistance them and . . . But he had gone over and over it in his mind, until the thing was perfect and little by little, secretly, he had made contact with those who would aid him. Stirling was loyal. Harry Stewart had arms there. To get there at the gallop, not even pausing at Lochleven, where Margaret Erskine lay . . .

He thought briefly of women, and the way in which

Angus, still standing behind him, had fed them to him to encourage his lust. He had been fourteen when he had taken his first maiden, a year ago and more. He knew well enough why Angus hoped to keep his mind on wenches, freeing it from any notion of responsibility so that he, the Red Douglas, would govern Scotland. They had interrupted his education, dismissed his beloved tutor Sir Davy Lindsay of the Mount, and replaced his thirst for knowledge with . . . fornication. He saw it plainly as if it were happening to someone else, not to him, the King. His mother had told him never to forget that he was royal. He loved his mother and liked Harry Stewart, the man who had replaced Angus in her bed and whom she now called her husband. When he was free he would make Harry a lord.

"When he was free . . . He thought of Margaret Erskine again: she attracted him with her thick dark brows and deep voice like a man's. With persuasion, he might get her to lie with him. Her husband was Sir James Douglas, a Douglas again . . .

"How fares my bonnie lad the day?"

The big old man had come in, and had walked over and put an arm about James' shoulders in the familiar way they all did, all the Douglases. This was old Kilspindie, whom in jest James had called Greysteel because he was so strong and ready, and could fight and tilt a lance and run like a boy. He was fond enough of Greysteel: but tomorrow he would be a Douglas like the rest. That was all. One must show no mercy. His uncle in England, great Henry VIII that his mother had told him of, showed none to offenders, breakers of the law. He hanged them, and knew no pity, and he was a great King. That was the model to copy.

He had answered Kilspindie absently, and the old man went back into the room to join his kin. They all three stood gossiping with their hands before their mouths, cautious lest he, James, should overhear. To stand like that, in

their monarch's very presence! Henry VIII would soon
have put them to the rightabout. But after tomorrow . . .
after the first dry day, he would see none of them again, not
brutal George nor sly Angus nor old wife Kilspindie. He
would hear no more of the half-sister Angus had got on his
mother, whom he did not know but disliked from that very
fact, the thought of Angus, the loathed, in bed with the
Queen.

If he had known, Angus had cast him a glance of
affection. He loved the son of the foolish, lustful woman he
had married in what seemed another life. He saw many
traits in James of his father, James IV. The lad wrote
poetry, some of it good, and was musical, more so than the
late King. He had no curiosity, as his father had had, about
experiments and dissecting and drawing teeth. In ways he
was more like his uncle in England, and, lest he emulate
that musical, poetic and ruthless monarch, Angus had
developed that other trait of James IV, the interest in
young women. A hot-blooded Stewart could be kept out of
mischief by the sight of fair breasts. And the boy must see
nothing of his mother. That was easy enough: Her Grace
was still taken up with Harry Stewart, and was again,
they said, pregnant by him. The divorce in Rome hung fire.
Oneself had to remember the rights of young Madge.
Madge's royal mother was spoilt, and had been even before
her famous bridal with James IV, for her father Henry VII
had let her do as she would after her mother's death. That
had still been so when he, Angus, married her, and had
tried at first to act as the late King had done, doing everything to please the Queen except abandon his mistresses.
But she was too wilful.

His mind had wandered accordingly to Janet of
Traquair, whom he had not troubled for some time. She
had lost her teeth and grown haggard, and still wore odd
clothes. Then George said something in his blunt way, and
Angus gave him his attention.

"Ay," said Kilspindie, nodding his head. The boy at the

window turned slowly, so that one could see his averted
greyhound profile, then his face.

He looks discontented, Angus thought. I must get him
another wench.

While I live, thought James V, they shall never find
refuge in Scotland.

He made himself smile and talk with them, as though
nothing untoward had been planned.

Next day was fine. The King rode out, Angus on one side of
him and George on the other. The collared hounds bayed,
horns sounded, hooves clattered, the hunt set off. There
was a fine stag ready-found in Falkland forest. James
made himself appear to be overcome by the excitement of
the chase, and spurred forward. But he would miss this
quarry. The trees swallowed him as they often did, and for
a time, he kept up the sound of shouting as though he
followed close. They heard his newly broken voice for a
while, then no longer. But they were not anxious, for they
would soon come up with him. All Stewarts loved the
chase.

But, except for Kilspindie, they were never to see him
again.

He had turned as he planned and galloped hard along the
forest paths. He knew them like his own hand. Soon he had
left the hunt behind, and the Douglases. He was free, free!
He pressed his horse and at last saw the blue water of a
loch under ths summer sky: Lochleven, with the castle
rearing in the midst, and he hardly thought of Margaret
Erskine.

Avoiding hamlets, so that they would not speak of his
direction, cutting through forest and field, road and ditch,
keeping to the wild, then woodland and more woodland, he
went. He must lose no time, for they would know by now
that he had run.

At one time he thought he heard them follow, and his

face whitened, but it was only a solitary farmer, plodding with his horse and cart to market. The market! Stirling itself would be the place! He was nearing it! He was near, and they had not hindered him!

But he never slackened speed until out of the flat Carse the castle could be seen, and the straggling houses of his father's ancient capital, rearing on the high Rock, with the sun piercing the clouds above it like rays about a crown. James prayed that they would be ready for him, and would open. To be taken now would break his heart.

But he galloped on, and at last rode up the slope. The folk knew him; there were welcoming faces at doors, and at last the Castle yard, and the great portcullis raised to let him enter, to see the grey buildings and the palace and the mint, and soldiers running to him, and handsome Harry Stewart ready to receive him. And the King dropped from his exhausted horse and embraced his mother's leman, then told them to shut the gate, and the great hinges creaked and he was home, and free.

"Ring down the portcullis! The King is come into his ain!"

He was King indeed. He would rule now as his father had done, and as his uncle did in England with no man to say him nay. The plan had borne fruit and the day was won. Linlithgow, Lennox' murder and their treatment of his own person, would be avenged. He, James the Fifth of Scotland, had sworn it.

"In ahint yon auld fail dyke
I wot there lies a new-slain knight;
And naebody kens that he lies there
Save his hawk, and his hound, and his lady fair."

William Lyon was cock-a-hoop for some reason; his lilting tongue sounded strange to her. It was as though he had power over her and knew it, though she swore to herself he had none. She made no answer, and turned away from where he stood, feeling the burning eyes follow her. Perhaps he was mad. If so he would destroy himself; but seeking for any reason to have him banished from Glamis, she found none.

15

The tidings filtered up from the south: the King had escaped and Angus was at a loss and had retired to Tantallon. Jonet pictured them all there; fierce Isobel, lashing her tongue at George; Kilspindie's town-bred wife, despised by the rest; young Margaret Douglas, putting away the needle quietly in her sewing to hear her father's news. Maybe nothing more would happen.

She waited anxiously for word from her brother. None came for Christmas, and none at Yule, which they celebrated quietly at Glamis, as deep snow had blocked the roads and guests could not come.

The snow thawed, and one day Jonet saw a rider coming might and main. It was Lord Forbes himself, leaving his retainers behind.

"My lady! My lady!" He had long come past the gallant stage with her: he loved her. He saw her fair face turn to him, the water-green eyes gazing clearly, and he blurted out his shocking news.

"My lady, ye had best make haste out of Glamis. The King has put all Douglases to the horn, among them yourself. None may succour or aid them on pain of death, or give them shelter. The King is besieging Tantallon and has taken heavy guns there, and dug ditches. Please God ye will be safe. Come with me, and bring the bairns. There is always a welcome in my house, and none will seek ye at Kynedward."

He was still breathing fast with the effects of his ride: he was not young. She remembered that before anything, even before she answered him.

"Surely the King's men will not ride so far north for a widow woman, who means His Grace no harm?"

"I tell ye, the thing is proclaimed at the very cross in
Forfar. Ye are attainted. For God's sake, get your gear,
and bring the bairns, and come with me."

"I cannot leave the servants in danger, and they will
protect me if need be." She still could not believe that it
would be needful: that boy of fifteen! And she herself had
done him no harm except to draw back when he had
fondled her breasts.

Lord Forbes spread out his hands. "The time is going
by while ye linger. Let little Elizabeth at any rate come:
at the least my son's bride will be out of harm's way with
us.

She sent for Elizabeth, saw to her gear, sent her back on
a pony with Lord Forbes and his men, who had now caught
up with him. It was pleasant that the child should be with
her bridegroom in their early years, and good of Lord
Forbes to offer it. Margaret refused to go with her sister:
she was stubborn, and would stay at Glamis.

When the party had gone off Jonet sent for Patrick
Charteris. He came, grave-faced. She already knew that
he had heard the tidings.

"Patrick, what are we to do? I told Lord Forbes that we
would stay here. But I would not wish harm to any of our
folk through the King's men. What ploy have ye?" She had
already had cause to have gratitude for his inventiveness
in difficulties, such as after Clang-Causey had died and
she was plagued with the man William Lyon. William still
showed himself, but kept a still tongue. She had confessed
her feeling against him to the priest, John Lyon, and
Father John had replied gently.

"He is one of God's creatures, as ye are, my lady: use him
as a soul for whom Christ has died."

But she had no time to think of William Lyon now.
Patrick remained before her, his loyal eyes burning with
anger at the news from the south.

"My lady, it were well maybe to leave Scotland for a
while, till His Grace's wrath should subside. He is but a

boy," he said.

She heard him as if her mind were harnessed to little wheels, which ran and ran.

"But we cannot," she told him, "leave without the King's writ, which governs Scotland."

"He will maybe not look at all things he signs. It is worth endeavour, Madam. Evil matter will come forth in the next few months, and ye are best out of harm's way."

"And the children?" She did not want to trespass on Forbes' hospitality. Elizabeth had been his care, but not the rest.

"God knows they have many great-aunts," said Patrick with a flash of humour. "Send them to my lady Ochterlony, or my lady Ross. The pity is that their grandmother is dead."

"But how long will the good ladies be troubled with them?" Within herself she thought of John and George, both young and uncertain. They needed their mother.

"We will see, Madam. But go ye must. We will find a way. Have I permission to write to His Grace, requesting a passport to France?"

France. King François Foxnose. The châteaux she had never seen, the places Angus had visited as ambassador, after Albany had had him shipped out of the kingdom drunk and drugged. France; the ancient ally of Scotland.

"Do what ye may," she said. "And, Patrick, ye maun bide with me. I would not know which way to ride without your help: ye are a right good servant."

He bowed, and hid beneath his eyelids such lust as William Lyon had almost openly proclaimed. But Patrick would never avow it, or give my lady discomfort because of it. She was so fair, so merciful!

He went to his own place in the castle and wrote at once to ask permission of the King to leave his kingdom, to any part except England. That was the constant enemy, and on no account to be visited, though they said my lord of

Angus, and his brother George, had already sent out enquiries there.

16

Attainder was in force against all of the Douglas clan by the spring of 1529. As Lord Forbes had foreseen, no man might give them shelter or aid them in any way under pain of death by the King's will and royal authority. Forbes had been brave enough in sheltering Elizabeth.

His Grace was still besieging Tantallon, although no one knew whether or not the great gun Mons would shoot her ten-pound ball, the size of a great loaf, with the rest among the rose-red arches and those parts that did not face the sea. The sea was the Douglases' sure hope and way of escape, if one must be found. But they held out bravely, even the child Margaret Douglas, who for the first time saw her half-brother, red hair flying—he had not yet cropped it—beyond the gate, riding up and down to encourage the men to fire their deafening volleys. The ditches he had dug upturned the green turf and it had become a red-brown mess of trodden earth. The days were an inferno and the nights full of fear. The Douglas men took turns to watch lest there should be an attempt to break through and enter in the dark.

The women were brave, but before the King tired of the command Tantallon was no place for them. One moonless night, young Madge and the rest descended the rock and were put in a boat, tilting against the waves, and small gear with them. The sound of the oars broke the silence. No one spoke, or wept. Madge craned her neck to see what would be the last sight she would ever have of Tantallon, but in the dark there was only blackness, rising against the sky. What was to become of her father? What was to become of herself? As long as the King did not lay hold of her to send her back to her mother, she would endure any misfortune, and knew it.

The men, including Huntly who had thrown in his lot with the Douglases, decamped a few days later, joining their women at a prearranged place. Angus had sent a quick letter off to Jonet, then had gone, his mouth grim. The boy he had loved was taking his revenge. The King was grown a man.

They stayed chiefly in the Border lands, so criss-crossed with bogs and warring loyalties that they were no more than one band of moss-troopers, living roughly like the rest. Hunted fugitives, wary of the King's men behind every hill, across marshes, behind whin-bushes, they lurked and hid, sleeping by night in barns and haystacks, often without the knowledge of the farm-hand in what was after all their own place, or had been before the King annexed all Douglas lands to himself. If tenants were faithful, it might well bring wrath down on the poor folk themselves. But many were so, giving food and shelter. If the worst befell, from here one could cross over into England. But then the Warden's men might well arrest or kill anyone in a brawl. It was a hard, bitter time for the man who had been the greatest lord in Scotland, more powerful than the King.

Angus was concerned for his daughter, Madge, who was fast becoming a woman and who showed rare courage and steadfastness towards him. For a while he lodged her at Norham, then Berwick. But the castellan of Berwick and his wife found the expense of keeping young Margaret Douglas and her women too great to bear, as Angus had frequently promised them money but had none. In the end her godfather, Cardinal Wolsey, was written to, begging that the girl might make her way to him in London. But the fate which seemed to hang over the Douglases prevented this: Wolsey had fallen from power, and could do nothing for anyone.

Madge rode down, not having waited to hear of it, and

came to London, and was welcomed at first by her uncle, Henry VIII, and made friends with his daughter, Mary. She was happy and secure for some years in the household of her aunt, the Queen-Duchess of Suffolk, and learned household lore and herbal knowledge there which would stand her in good stead in later years, when she married none other than the son of the murdered favourite of James V, Matthew, Earl of Lennox. Madge was to bear him many children, most of whom died. Her whole life was spent in rigorous poverty, for she was a stern Catholic and as such out of favour with every monarch except Queen Mary in her brief reign.* Madge's surviving elder son made a brilliant marriage, and then was lost: his name was Henry, Lord Darnley.

But Madge for the time, now, had put away all thoughts of comfort, all memories of neat embroidery and timely meals. Sometimes, when pressure was hard, Angus would again take her across Tweed to the care of the castellan of Norham and his wife, but it was not much more comfortable in that castle, whose walls dripped damp, than in the open. In any case Madge longed to be with her father, danger or none, and would rejoin him as soon as she might.

Jonet in the far north was their mainstay. She had busied herself at once, after Tantallon fell, in sending great cheeses and salted beef, blankets and warm hose. Patrick Charteris himself often rode to the Border with the gear, and brought back news: the Earl had grown a heavy beard to disguise himself, and might be taken for any poor ragged man: and the Lady Margaret's fair skin was burned black as a gipsy's with living under the sky. George's bastard son was with them, and George himself. There was no knowing from day to day who would be taken by night.

At last Angus did a thing which he had long been

* See *The Green Salamander.*

unwilling to do, for his daughter's sake. Her mother's divorce had lately been granted, and there was danger of Madge's being declared a bastard and no heir. Angus set his teeth and rode down into England, leaving Madge well guarded at Berwick. He went to beg of Henry VIII, who it was known did not approve of his sister's actions, and, now Harry Stewart had been made Lord Methven by King James, called him my lord Muffin. Angus risked his neck or his head, and exercised all his charm on great Harry of England.

Fortunately, the King took to him and thereafter defended him in every way, regarding him always as his sister Margaret's lawful husband and agreeing to take the waif of a girl, Madge, to be looked after by her young aunt, the Duchess of Suffolk. Mary Tudor had been, for a brief while, Queen of France, then her old husband had died—they said she danced him into his grave—and she, to Henry VIII's wrath, had promptly married the man she loved, Charles Brandon, the King's boon companion. Brandon as Duke of Suffolk was less thick about the King than he had been. He and his royal wife were somewhat coldly treated still, for it had lost the goodwill of France to have acted as they had done. But Duchess Mary did not greatly care: she excelled in all housewifely tasks, and loved to look after her great bear of a husband, struggling in fact with poverty and attaining much knowledge of herbs, meats and embroidery. Madge Douglas would learn all these arts from her, and to the end of her long existence be a good housewife.

But to be separated again from Angus caused his daughter grief. And Angus was now in English pay, making forays from the south on Border lands, with George by him. James V had not reckoned on his royal uncle's support for the hated Earl, and grew bitter by reason of it: it spoiled his kingship. But Huntly, whom he loved, soon returned to him and was forgiven.

Now Jonet was free of care for her brother, and made

haste to cross overseas, Patrick Charteris with her.

She took the King's written pass in her bodice, and kept close to Patrick on the ride. William Lyon had elected to travel with them to the port, and she could not prevent him, although they had had words when William learnt of the journey. He had edged up to her as he always did, and Jonet as usual had downed her dislike of the man. As the old priest had said, William was a Christian soul. He tried again to wheedle her into marriage.

"Ye are without protection. On this very journey—" He had been angered about the journey, not having thought to get himself a pass abroad, "—any man may throw ye in a ditch, and none will succour an attainted rebel. It is folly to attempt a ride across country. At Glamis ye are safe, with me."

She answered him gently, as she had long made herself do.

"I have said it before, William, and I say it again: I have love for ye as a Christian soul, but not as a man." Never as a man. She could hardly bear to look upon him, and his appearance had changed little over the years; he was still what the Scots call sleekit.

When she and Patrick took ship she saw William still standing uselessly on shore, unable to follow. His solitary figure aroused pity in her: he should rid himself of his obsession which brought neither him nor herself happiness.

Patrick Charteris came quietly with a warm cloak he had taken from the baggage; the April breeze was cold, and he put it round her. She laid a hand on his sleeve.

"Patrick, I am glad of ye," she told him. It was not the first or second time she had said it, but it pleased him. His love for her was as different from William's as anything could be, never presuming, never wearying her.

The voyage was smooth, and she saw the coast of France for the first time: it looked like the Border land of Scotland, green and flat.

They disembarked at the port and she grew used to hearing the swift brittle sound of French spoken everywhere: she knew some, as all Scots of any position did. The old ally was still preferred to England.

They rode through the strange new country, seeing the fields planted lilac with young flax. The inns were comfortable, their food good and the beds clean. Why did foreigners always do so much better in these ways than folk at home? The cooking interested Jonet, with its use of mushrooms and garlic. Garlic at home grew wild, with small white flowers. When would they win back to Glamis, and savour the scent? But it was too soon to think of that. As far as she knew the King's wrath had not followed his proclamation at Forfar; the two boys, Johnny and George, and dour Margaret, were being cared for by Uncle John at Innerpeffray, and Margaret Drummond's daughter would be there, and would mother them.

And the King? Perhaps, if he had thought about the matter at all, he expected her to stay abroad. But his anger was quick and had maybe spent itself.

She journeyed to Amiens, where her grandfather had often come on pilgrimage. The sight of the great cathedral astonished her, surrounded by windmills and dyers' houses like puppies about a bitch. Inside, the soaring pillars took their flight from the stone floor, worn by the knees of many pilgrims. The colours of the famous rose window were spilled on the floor, the sun behind them: and lit candles blazed about the Chapel of St. Sauve. Jonet knelt at all the shrines, and touched the reliquary of St. Formin, the beheaded saint, rich with gold and jewels. She prayed for Angus, for George, and for the soul of Clang-Causey. She prayed also for the young King of Scots, that he might rid himself of hate; hate was a destroyer, and James V unprotected. It seemed a long time that she knelt there, unnoticed among the other pilgrims, clad like them in hood and cloak. Then she came out into the April sunlight.

Patrick was waiting; he had remained at the back of the cathedral, eyes fixed on her. Kate, who had come with them, stared at Charteris. It was a long time now since she had fallen in love with him, but he had no eyes for anyone but my lady; and why should he not, when my lady was so fair, and she, Kate Lyon, so ugly?

They took ths road to Blois, where Jonet would meet the King and maybe put in a word for her brothers that would be returned to young King James.

17

King James himself was riding that summer through his King's Park of Stirling, with young Huntly by him having come down from the north. They cantered past the trees, the fences, His Majesty's father had planted and raised in his time. Above them was the Ladies' Lookout, where long ago the Queen and her women had stood laughing to watch the Abbot of Tongland sail out above the sharp descent on the pair of giant wings the King had made from birds' feathers, to try to prove that man could fly. But the wings had only been caught by the wind and when that dropped had cast the Abbot down among the woods with a broken leg. James recalled the tale: his mother had told him of it. He wished, not for the first time, that he had known his father. Now that his will was obeyed he could feel it thrusting ahead of him, forcing him to actions which later, in silence, he would repent. But no one must know of that.

"Someone is kneeling over there," said Huntly. It was the figure of an old man, his beard long, grey, and catching the sunlight. He had the forlorn attitude of a suppliant.

James narrowed his eyes. "I believe," he said, "that that is old Kilspindie." How dared any Douglas, even one of whom he had been fond, defy his edict to dwell forth of Scotland! He let out his rein, and rode past the kneeling old man without as much as a look, a gesture. No one should think him a weakling: it was as well to appear firm, to be as good as his word.

The riders disappeared into the trees and the old man rose unsteadily to his feet. It was a hot day and he was not mounted, and as a precaution wore a shirt of mail under his tunic. The sight of the red-haired boy on the horse had unmanned him. Had James indeed forgotten his fondness

for him, Greysteel, for his ploys and his stories, and their
games of strength?

He went on, at last ascending the Castle hill past the
place where the King had ridden up. At the gate he sank
down, exhausted.

"Give me, I pray you, a drink of water," he said to the
guard.

The man stared stolidly ahead and did not move.
Kilspindie's grey head sank in the heat. Towards evening
he staggered up and went away.

The King in time heard of his request, and that no man
would so much as give Kilspindie a drink of water. Indeed
his own power was strong in the land now. Men saw that
his word was his bond: no Douglas was free of Scotland any
more. He had not rested till the brood were rooted out.
They should never have even the shadow of power again,
and he had shown that day that when it was a struggle
between law and affection, the law won. He would go on
thus, and be better than his father, as good as his uncle in
England; ay, as good as that, deserving the new title of
Majesty.

18

The Court of France moved between Blois and Amboise, both being palaces the King was rebuilding after the Italian wars. Queen Claude had died as quietly as she had lived, and Jonet made her curtsy to the new Queen, Eleanor of Austria, formerly Queen of Portugal. The poor woman was not loved by anyone here, least of all her husband. Her presence had been one of the conditions of peace between her brother the Emperor and King François, and every time he looked at her the King thought of his own defeat and long imprisonment in Madrid. Eleanor was a beautiful woman, but without humour or wit, which would have endeared her to the King of France. She spent her time sadly and patiently as his first wife had done, at her prayers or sewing with her women. She and Jonet had little to say to one another, as Eleanor's French was scanty and Jonet spoke it as the Scots did, fluently enough but with an accent.

With the King it was different. Jonet saw his small lecherous eyes rove over her, and the incredibly long broad nose quiver, as though he followed a scent which pleased him.

"You are the sister of milord Angus, Madame," he said, and made one or two kindly remarks about the time Angus and George had spent as ambassadors by the Regent's writ.

That same Albany, his beard beginning to turn grey, and famous now for his guerrilla war against the Emperor while the King was held captive, stood close by the King, and came to kiss Jonet's hand. Afterwards he guided her about Court. There was a sadness about him, as if he could not join with any heart in card-playing and dancing, though the viols played.

"I still mourn my wife," he said. "I left Scotland for her sake, which perhaps I should not have done so soon. I believe things are quiet there at present." He cast a glance at her cautiously. One had best not say overmuch about the King's outlawry of the Douglases.

"Quiet enough," she said, and they went on to talk of other things. Albany showed her the gardens, still in infancy yet, and marred by the great piles of pallid stone and rubble which were building.

"The King saw palaces in Italy which fired his fancy, and nothing will do but that all the old palaces must be pulled down and new ones built," said the Duke. "Every lord, naturally, wants to copy the King, so everyone is building classic fronts, arches and twisting staircases. It will cost a deal of money, but when it is done it will be beautiful, no doubt.

"Turn about here, Madame, and you will see the great new front. There is to be a staircase built, twisting on and up."

She turned, and admired the new style of the King's building, also the equestrian statue of dead Louis XII over the door. But what interested her more were two figures, a woman and a child, walking in the gardens.

"That is the King's sister *la Reine Marguérite* with young Madame Madeleine," said Albany. "Let us pay our respects to them. At one time it was talked of that this child might marry your King."

The little girl was delicate as a fairy, shining in her jewelled gown. She smiled, showing a new second tooth. Jonet curtsied to her and to Marguérite de Valois, Queen of Navarre, the King's sister, famed for her wisdom and learning. The little girl tugged at her aunt's skirt. Behind her the roses were in bud already.

"*Madame ma tante*, may I please pick a rosebud? Please."

"She wants everything with such intensity," said

Marguérite, as the little princess ran off. "I fear that she may be hurt by the world, but which of us are not?"

Madeleine came back crying, with a bud in her hand.

"It has pricked me," she said.

"Yes, my child," replied Marguérite, bending to look at the small bleeding finger. "It will heal soon. In life one meets thorns as well as roses." She took a delicate handkerchief and dabbed at the blood. "There, do not cry. It is better, and you have your rose. We must go and put it in water quickly. Make your curtsy to my lady Glamis."

Madeleine curtsied, swiftly and gracefully, her delicate fingers still holding the rose.

"Madame, may I kiss her?" Jonet asked. She loved the pretty child. Everyone must surely feel love for her at sight. How would she fare in rough Scotland, if she ever travelled as far?

She kissed the peach-smooth cheek.

"May God go with you, Madame," she said, and watched the pair walk away.

Albany was still beside her, smiling a little. "She would make a bonnie Queen," he said. "But her mother was consumptive, and so are her sisters. It is not time for a formal betrothal yet."

"The King would delight in her when she is a little older." One could picture James, who so loved jewels and splendour, being entranced by the beautiful little girl when she should be a woman. But all that was to come, maybe. Foreign alliances blew hot and cold.

"I will take you to another countryman, a little older this time," said Albany. He led her to where two young boys sat on a stone, playing cards. The sunlight glinted on their fair hair. They stood up, and made their bow.

"This," said Albany, "is Matthew, Earl of Lennox, and his brother."

Jonet flushed a little, remembering the murder of their father, the King's friend, at Linlithgow. The elder boy must be about thirteen by now. His close-set blue eyes regarded her without expression. He knows, she thought, who I am.

She tried to ease matters. "What will you do when you are grown, my lords?" she said. Matthew Stewart answered, shortly and without more talk.

"I at least will enter the Scots Archers of the Guard of France. My brother may do what he will."

The other boy smiled blandly. He was stout and looked lazy and dull.

"The white and gold livery will look well on you," said Jonet in French. "I am glad, my lord, that we have met."

He did not answer, and Albany led her inside the palace, from which there came the sounds of music; the Court was still dancing. She was not to know that she had met the bridegroom of Madge Douglas.

The King and the Dauphin were both in the dance. François was wildly joyous at this time, making every moment of his freedom after so long in the Emperor's Spanish prison. His two sons had in the end been sent as hostages, to replace him, but had been freed on the King's marriage to widowed Eleanor, only the elder, the brilliant Dauphin François, had died shortly after coming home. Henri, the second brother, looked always as if he knew he was less beloved, less talented, less witty than his brother and all of it weighed him down. His eyes followed a young girl who was dancing. Jonet found out that her name was Diane de Poitiers, and that she had an elderly husband who was not present today.

"Both King and Dauphin are in love with her," murmured Albany. "Do you care to dance, Madame?"

"No, I had best watch, being a widow." She stood aside and surveyed the Court of France. The King danced with his mistress Anne Duchesse d'Etampes, who had been the first person sent to him on his release from prison. She was slight and fair-haired, and moved gracefully in her blue velvet gown and matching hood trimmed with pearls.

Albany forbore to whisper that Anne had the pox and had given it to the King, or that she was said to be a Huguenot: walls had ears.

The King and his mistress stopped again by them, and Jonet was made known to the Duchesse, whose knowing blue eyes scanned her.

"Do you stay with us long, Madame de Glamis?" she asked quietly.

Jonet answered gently. "No, Madame. I have been on pilgrimage to Amiens to pray for the soul of my husband, and will return to Scotland as soon as I may."

"That is a pity. The King would like you to remain here."

"Madame, I have children at home."

Anne de Heilly shrugged. "They can be looked after. Remain with us for a little; do you not admire the new building here? There are other places also. You must see the little châteaux on the water, where we have water-parties, and come to watch the hunt start in the mornings. There are forests here; the Brush Wood, the Moat Wood, the rest. It is a fine sight."

Jonet was looking at the plaster wrought ceiling, with the initials F and C for François and Claude, patterned everywhere. She thought of a thing to say. "I see the salamander often," she said. The fabled beast was constantly recurring, over doorways, over hearths, below mantels.

"That is the King's crest," said the Duchesse, smiling.

"It is the Douglas crest also, but ours spouts flames."

"We must tell that to the King. He will be interested. He knew your brothers some years ago, when they were here. The Earl of Angus is very handsome."

"You are kind, Madame." She did not know whether or not it was etiquette to be seen in close company with the King's mistress; but perhaps it was different here. She let the Duchesse lead her through the palace, admiring the newly painted rooms. At the end there was a small closet with a *prie-dieu*, surmounted with a Spanish triptych.

"That is the Queen's." And out of a doorway stepped King François himself, having left the dancing. He came over and bowed to the Duchesse, then took Jonet's arm.

"I have many things also to show our fair Scottish guest," he said. And Anne de Heilly curtsied and went.

Jonet stayed at Blois meantime; they were hospitable, and seemed to like her company. The King himself she found amusing and it was pleasant to laugh again. His sister also was witty, as well as learned. Jonet became familiar with the famed widow's peak of Marguérite, below which her white forehead would ponder many things. She loved her brother, and the two of them would laugh and joke by the hour together, and as often as not in these days Jonet would be with them, by invitation. She had Kate dress her in her grandest gear, and bought a pair of new sleeves in raised figured velvet. It was pleasant to be able to wear magnificent clothes and hear good talk; Glamis seemed far away, bleak, and lonely.

One day the King took her into the gardens. They could talk openly with one another now; she regarded him as a friend, and the notable nose in his shrewd face amused her secretly. He was as different from old King Louis XII as it was possible to be; there was still a saying that the old King used to go to bed with the chickens. His lined, anxious face peered out now and again from portraits, and Jonet wondered how young Mary Tudor, Her Grace of Scotland's younger sister, had liked being married to Louis. At any rate there was that saying that she had danced him into his grave; and then François, as the next heir, had come.

He led her about the gardens in silence; his famous peach-coloured roses preened themselves on the terraces, and beyond that again the vineyards were in full leaf. Presently he spoke, in a low voice so that none of the courtiers, strolling about in their peacock finery, could hear.

"Madame de Glamis, I am desolate for love of you. Have a little pity on me."

"Sire, you speak in jest." She was so accustomed to his company by now that she believed this, although the jest was a bad one. She flushed, while the small bright eyes regarded her.

"I do not jest. Remain here with us, and I will give you a little château where you can be alone, if you wish, till I come. You may have your children with you. Picture to yourself how much better it would be than in Scotland, where I hear the King pursues your family to the death."

For instants she thought of it; the little château, and Johnny and George and Margaret and Elizabeth free to run about in the warm sunshine; and freedom from fear. Yet it was not for her. She answered gently, not leaving hold of the King's arm in its puff-slashed sleeve.

"Sire, I am a Douglas, and Douglas women do not lend themselves to dishonour." She did not know of James V's mistress, Margaret Erskine, the wife of Lochleven.

He flushed, the colour coming up from his narrow shirt-frill to the sharp-featured face above the thick neck. "Madame de Glamis," he said, "I beg of you to consider my proposal. At home, in Scotland, there is nothing for you or for your children: I have ascertained it. Here they could win honour as M. the Duc d'Aubigné has done by his energies in the late war." He pronounced the French form of Albany. "My good friend Anne d'Etampes," he said, "has been married to an old courtier to preserve her status as a married woman. M. d'Aubigné would agree to the same arrangement, I am certain. He mourns his dead wife, and would not trouble you."

"Sire, it is not a question which I could ever consider. You have my answer. It will not change."

He bowed, red-faced, at last over her hand; and turned and left her alone with the sight and scent of the roses.

She had been troubled lest the matter should lose her the friendship of Madame Marguérite, the King's sister; but that lady came to her, smiling as though nothing had happened.

"You spoke of a salamander spouting flames," she said. "Our good Berthelot, the King's chamberlain, has a divine little château at Azay-le-Rideau, where he has carved such animals out of compliment to the King. I should like you to see it with me. We could travel by litter; it is more than a day's ride."

Jonet accepted, glad to be rid of Court for a little while; no doubt if she went away King Francois would forget her. She smiled at *la reine Margot*. "I should be happy to come, Madame," she said.

They set out the next day; the litter was full of embroidered cushions and made private by brocade curtains which could be drawn close. Marguérite made witty conversation all the way. Jonet gazed out on the green summer countryside of France; the flax in the fields was turning to the colour of lavender. One did not see it at home. They would stop to pick wild strawberries in the woods, and relieve themselves; once they stopped overnight at a great house filled with painted ceilings, and then rode on to Azay-le-Rideau itself. Jonet exclaimed with delight at the little white château surrounded by its moat, with water-lilies floating. They saw the salamander above the doorway.

"We will rest here," said Marguérite. They had not brought Kate or the other servants; Monsieur Berthelot, evidently, would provide all such needs as doing honour to his King's sister when she chose to visit his domain. They descended from the litter, and until dinner was ready walked about the grounds, seeing themselves reflected in the moat. Jonet did not know her own reflection; was this fashionable personage, with frizzed hair and earrings, herself?

They dined well and then went to bed, Jonet having her hair combed out by a strange maid. She wondered where M. Berthelot was and whether it cost him dear to leave his house to others. No one in Scotland that she knew would have tolerated such visits in the absence of the host. But things were different here.

She was in her shift, her hair combed out to its full length; the maid had left. As she saw herself in a mirror, a man climbed out from behind the clothes-chest. It was the King. Jonet cried out at sight of him and he laid a finger over his lips.

"Do not wake them," he said, smiling. "Ah, Madame, you would not give yourself to me, and so I have come to you. You are driving me mad with desire."

"Sire, I have given you my answer, as I said."

"Madame, here you have no choice." He had approached her and was fingering the soft locks of her hair, her arms, her breasts. She jerked away.

"Ye may force me," she said in Scots, "if ye wish. I have no doubt the servants here are trained not to hear women screaming. Ye are stronger than I. But can ye think for one moment, sire, that such a situation could continue if I do not wish it? I would leave here and leave France, and publish your dishonour to the world. For it would be yours, not mine." She heard the French spill easily from her again: she had regained mastery of herself.

"You are hard, Madame," he said. He had drawn back.

"Not hard, but honourable. A king may have all his desires met, except those which will not willingly be granted."

"You persist in this?" His eyes scanned her. By now, she was thinking, I could have been the mistress of three kings; Henry of England, James of Scotland, and now the King of France. She stood unyielding, while he drew back from her; his face was downcast.

"I could take you, as you say," he said, "but I will not. *Excusez-moi.*"

The door slammed behind him, and Jonet sank down on the bed. If only Patrick Charteris had been here, to lie all night outside her door, or Kate on a pallet! She could not believe that she would be left in peace.

But the King did not return. He rode through the night to Blois, thinking of ways to redeem his pride. By dawn a solution came to him; he would take Berthelot's château, where Jonet Douglas had dismissed him, for his own. The salamanders had been carved in honour to him; now they would be his, and despite himself he would remember always that the woman who had flouted him had been a Douglas, and proud as the devil.

My lady Glamis was coming home. William Lyon received the word, staring out of the castle window to where the leaves showed dull with autumn. His mind was full of the thing he had done, long months ago now. He had been full of mortified anger when she took Patrick Charteris to France and not himself. How faithful he had been over the years, yet she would not be gracious to him! She would catch sight of him, and cast a gentle word such as she did to other folk; nothing more.

He had ridden, when all was said, after her departure for France, down to Stirling and had been admitted to the King, very grand in a suit of white velvet. Since Angus' going James could spend as much as he liked on clothes, or on anything.

He had let William Lyon kiss his hand, but the man did not at first interest him. In James' mind was a late adventure, when, as he now loved to do, he had disguised himself as a common person, and had slipped out of the castle gate on to the Ballengeich road, and wandered about listening and watching ordinary folk. He would do it often; a monarch must know what the people of his kingdom were doing and saying, and he had a taste for the common man, and woman. The Gudeman of Ballengeich, that was what he called himself when any asked: the name amused him.

He returned his gaze to the man who had come from Glamis. What was he saying? Some matter about the châtelaine, who was Angus' sister. She had aided the rebels with food, blankets, hose, eh? He must again take note of Lady Glamis' doings. Yet at present she was out of the country, and no doubt would not return. But if she did, perhaps a show of power, lest she come to think of herself as forgotten? A Douglas, who had once rejected him, here in this very place! Certainly she should not be left in idle enjoyment of her acres.

"Ye are welcome here," he said to William Lyon. "A loyal man is meat and drink. Return from time to time, and inform me of everything that takes place at Glamis after your lady returns, if she intends to."

"Sire, she must mean it, for her children are still in Scotland." He was unable to implicate Innerpeffray: he did not know where the children had been sent, as it was kept a secret except for those concerned, and William was not one of these.

The voyage home was uneventful, England's coasts being seen in a haze of distance, but nobody challenged the ship. Jonet had wrapped herself in a cloak on deck, Patrick Charteris by her. She stared out at the grey sea and wondered if she would have accepted King François' terms if he had been prepared to aid her brother. The King of France had preserved a discreet silence on the subject of Angus and the King of Scots.

She turned to Patrick; there was a thing she had often wanted to say to him, and now, with Kate in the cabin alone, was the moment. It had not been difficult to guess at Kate's love for the good servant. He stood tall and dark against the day, and for an instant it crossed Jonet's mind that she herself had never looked on him as a man, with a man's lusts.

"Patrick, I would have a word with ye. Why do ye not take a wife?"

He flushed. "There has no one come my way, my lady, that I could marry." It was as near the truth as he dared say it; she must never know that she herself was all that was beautiful and desirable to him, her servant. Looking at her now against the churning sea with her hair blowing from its coif, her eyes wide, he could almost have told his love; but he said nothing and never would.

"There is Kate," said his lady. "She would make a good wife for a man. She is loyal and honest, and not a fool. She is too greatly ashamed of her looks; if ye were to marry her, and be good to her, she would repay it well." But he had turned away, and they said no more of Kate. In due time they sighted Scotland, and Jonet remembered the two letters she had had in France, from her brothers, saying the King's anger had not abated; they wrote from makeshift hiding-places since having had to quit Tantallon.

But it was good to be home again; her heart had warmed within her at sight of the Scottish coast grey in the distance, and then nearing, and the brisk Scots voices of the pilot and crew. Nothing had changed, nor ever would, here; and the ride north was prevented by nobody. In spite of everything she was thankful to see the towers of Glamis again; it was her home, and she felt a sensation rise in her she had not known before. Glamis, her home; some folk had none. She loved it, not only for its towers and its grandeur. Here was the place she had made her own, where she had brought up her children. She would be glad to embrace them again.

The children had been brought back from Innerpeffray, and had grown tall. Her baggage was unloaded, the gifts she had brought for them from France causing pleasure to Margaret especially, for although there was a doll for

Elizabeth, who would soon return to the Forbeses, their mother had brought a French tapestry for Margaret with a unicorn on it. It was as if it made known that Margaret was no longer a child, and unlike anybody else. The girl held it up and brooded over it for a long time, mouth smiling as it seldom did. It was well seen she was the daughter of Clang-Causey.

"It shall hang in my chamber, where I can see it from my bed," said Margaret, and smoothed the rich stuff of the hanging. She loved her tapestry: it was a possession she would always cherish through the difficult years.

By evening Jonet was weary, and sought her bed. Kate came to undress her and to comb her hair. It was a relief to get out of the stiff bodice and laced sleeves, and into her shift. Just then the woman gave a loud cry, and pointed. A pair of feet showed beneath the window-curtain. She ran across, and jerked the curtain wide. William Lyon stood there, his pale eyes fixed on Jonet. Another few moments and he could have been in her bed.

"Get out, ye dirty carline! Out, I say! Out!" Kate gave him a blow across the mouth, and fled from the room, calling for Patrick Charteris.

"Be silent," Jonet bade her, wrapping her own bedgown close. It were best that the whole household should not hear. She faced William. It was the episode at Azay-le-Rideau all over again.

"I have had patience," she said, "but now it is at an end. From this day ye will not enter Glamis. I shall give orders to the gatemen. Take yourself to your own place, and bide there."

"My place is in hell," he said, and fell at her knees. "Do not banish me. Ye are my life. How has the time gone by for me while ye were in France? Every hour I thought, 'She is in talk with some other man, who will not love her as I do.' " He began to weep, and Jonet moved back from him.

"Go from here," she said, and Charteris appeared in the doorway. He seized William by the arm and said, "Come with me."

The man went, in silence. Jonet found that she was trembling. She made sure that William was out of the castle before she sought her bed, and weary as she was, she did not sleep that night.

There had been no further word of the attainder. No doubt the King had some new thing to occupy him, notably Margaret Erskine, who was said to be with child by him. Jonet settled back into her household duties, relieved to know that Angus and George were now safe in London, at the English court.

19

She had two years in peace. There were proposals of marriage from several local noblemen. She did not accept them. She took pleasure in her house, the more now William was gone from it. For the rest, there was always hospitality to be found at Glamis. She grew famous for her sweet bed-linen and well-cooked food, and she planted a little herb-garden so that she might try French cooking as she had known it in that country. Margaret helped her weed the thyme and fennel and lavender, which last did not grow too well in the cold north. Sometimes Elizabeth would come from Innerpeffray to visit them, escorted by her uncle and her young betrothed. The pair were already happy together, and it was pleasant to see the dark head and the fair bent close, examining a flower, a book. The Master of Forbes was turning into a handsome young fellow, and gentle. Jonet knew Elizabeth would be content with him. Innerpeffray was already the girl's home.

The aunts called often at Glamis, and related gossip north and south. It was known that the King of England no longer cared for his new wife Anne.

"She has borne him but one living child, a daughter," mumbled Lady Ochterlony, managing her false shark's teeth, which did not fit. "Strange it will be if our old Queen is copied by her brother with divorces! May God forbid, and may our own King have a happy bridal. He is more than the age for it."

Jonet thought for a moment of the Queen, who was at Methven Castle in Perthshire, living still with Harry Stewart and the son and daughter she had borne him, but it was said they were bickering. Yet the King favoured Lord Methven, knowing that he could manage the ageing, plaintive Queen better than anyone. She had lately been known to declare that Angus was still her husband, and that foretold trouble. At the time of the divorce she had given as one of her reasons the statement that James IV was still alive, and had not been killed at Flodden but was leading the hidden life of a monk, which was most unlikely.

News filtered north with the pack-carriers, with whom Jonet did not speak. But the aunts did, and kept her fed with the doings at the English Court, where her brother was still a favourite, and now enjoyed a pension from King Henry. Jonet wondered how young Madge Douglas would fare in a place of shifting loyalties. If she had known, Madge was in utmost danger. Even the King had not foreseen that if he divorced his Queen, and declared their daughter Elizabeth illegitimate, Margaret Douglas was the next heir to the throne. She had made matters worse by falling in love with Lord Thomas Howard, a kinsman of that Duke of Norfolk who had fought at Flodden. Soon enough the King saw the true position of affairs, separated the lovers and clapped them in the Tower.

"The poor lass," said Jonet when she heard. "If the Queen were a loving mother she would write to King Henry, pleading her daughter's cause and offering to take her home. But I doubt if she will."

To do her justice, Queen Margaret did. It was the first time in years that she had mentioned her Douglas daughter's name. Now she wrote with firmness to her royal brother, telling him to send Madge north to her, "who would not have been disherst had she been with me." This referred to the dread Angus had long had of his daughter's being declared bastard at the time of Her Grace's divorce. But in any event King Henry took no heed: he had enough trouble with his sister in supplying her with money in exchange for information about what went on in Scotland. But Cardinal Wolsey, who had arranged it, would not be powerful much longer, and news of his fall surprised no one, although older folk remembered the able, blue-jowled young churchman who had ridden north in the time of James IV, with word from England.

Madge Douglas was freed after a year and sent to the convent of Syon. Her lover was dead of fever in the Tower. But soon all convents would suffer a like fate with Wolsey, and the solitary girl was brought back to Court then, waiting on Queen Anne Boleyn, which she found unpleasant. She had been a staunch friend of the Princess Mary, whose name now was never spoken. As for Queen Catharine, she still refused to call herself anything but the King's true wife, and was accordingly sent from one prison to another.

At Glamis they heard the news with disbelief: great folk did not act so, and Angus' letters were so circumspect they said nothing of it.

But by then, Jonet had been called to face a jury.

20

Armed men had come in the bitter January weather, defiling out of the winter trees. Their leader was a man named Gavin Hamilton, one of Arran's many bastard sons. He had entered with his following before anyone thought to stop them. The hall of Glamis was suddenly filled with men, the firelight shining on their cuirasses and swords, and the yard outside full of jostled horses.

Jonet came down.

"Who may ye be?" she asked. "We do not thole rough manners here." The men spat on the floor and one of them scratched himself.

Gavin, who had a brutal face, came forward.

"Ye are Lady Glamis?"

"I am, but I know ye not."

"I am Gavin Hamilton, to whom the King has given power of escheat. I am to take all your goods, Madam, and the movables."

His eyes fell before her gaze: he had not expected her to be so beautiful. She was wearing a green winter gown of camlet, and the lovesome shape of her body unmanned him. Surely the King's Grace—one still called him so though he had desired, like his uncle, to be called Majesty—was mistaken? This was no rebel: a quiet, agreeable lady, going about her business in this well-kept place. He felt ashamed of his late speech and said, "Madam, ye are put to the horn these two year past. I do but obey the King in coming here."

"The property is not mine, but my son's." The young lord had followed his mother. He was not notable, thought Gavin. The lady had put her arm about Johnny, as if to strengthen him in face of an enemy.

"I know not. I was told to come. It is a bitter day, and my men thirst." He would not, he knew, have the heart to rip down these hangings, seize the silver flagons, ruin her hall.

"Your men shall quench their thirst, if ye will go away."

"My lady, the King will be wroth."

"My son and I are loyal to the King. He has no cause to be wroth with us." She gestured to a servant, who brought, bewildered, the last brewing of small-ale, and some bread and meats. The men ate and drank greedily, and after they had gone there would be a scrubbing.

Gavin Hamilton stayed by my lady, who kept her countenance. He found himself more and more in love with her, forgetting his wife at home.

He went at last, but only after telling Jonet that she must face a jury in a month's time.

"Who are the jury?" she asked.

"The gentry of hereabouts."

She smiled, despite her unease. The gentry of hereabouts would never pronounce against her.

She rode to the court hearing with Innerpeffray, who was her cautioner. It was February, and the snow had melted and frozen and melted again, leaving grey slush. She dismounted from her horse and put her hood back, and went into the hall. There was nobody there but an usher. He came forward and bowed.

"Where is the jury?" Jonet asked him. She was uncertain of her charge. The whole matter was ridiculous.

"My lady, they have not appeared. They will not come now: the hearing was fixed for noon."

She went back to Glamis, having encountered no jury. Later Lord Forbes rode in.

"There could not," he said, "be found anyone who would serve, or declare against ye."

So she stayed at Glamis.

William Lyon had audience again of the King. That personage was grown, and had broadened a little. They said his son by Margaret Erskine was a black dour devil, like his mother, but the King was proud of him and had called him James, created Earl of Moray. The secret Tudor eyes beheld William, skulking in his riding-clothes with a shirt of mail beneath.

"The late jury would not obey my order? They shall be fined," said the King. "Have ye more to say? This woman is obdurate, and must be punished." He heard his own voice loud in the chamber. Those who would not conform to his will would feel his anger, like his uncle's. That uncle had not been pleasant of late, though he had sent James the Garter and it gleamed now on his leg and his chest.

William bowed his head. "Sire, the late Lord Glamis died gey sudden."

"Indeed so? Could his lady have bidden him Godspeed?"

"That I do not know, Sire. I only say what all men speak of." He was lying, and knew it.

James fingered his St. George, dropping his eyelids. He was dressed like a great prince, and his hair had been cropped above his ears in the new fashion.

"If all men speak, the jury must find her guilty. We will take one not from her immediate neighbours, as before, but from a wider net. They will not refuse my order."

But the second jury, like the first, refused, despite the fines. Not all of them had met Jonet Glamis, but all knew her fame and that it was fair. It was only her Douglas blood the King had against her. Everyone in four counties was sure of that.

She had felt her blood go back to her heart in shock: a charge at last of poisoning Clang-Causey? She had not loved him, but she had never hated him: and to think of such a thing was itself alien. She wondered if the physician she had called in at Leith was still to be found: he would testify for her, surely. And yet . . . that taut belly, that grey face, might have come there by poison, and no man could deny.

"God knows I would never have given it him," she murmured aloud. Fear came to her, and she tried to put it aside like other weakness. She was a Douglas, and must act as those of her blood, bravely, never flinching. What would the King do now?

The King did nothing meantime: he was shortly engrossed with an important matter, his own marriage.

21

Marriage was in the air. It had been arranged that Elizabeth Lyon would wed the Master of Forbes in June. The day was fine, and for the first time in many months Jonet felt free of persecution. Perhaps it was because much-married old Lord Forbes gave her his arm at sight and led her into his new castle of Kynedward, with the plaster still smelling damp on its dressed chamber walls. Then there was the sight, always welcome, of many friends, dressed bravely today in slashed sleeves and velvet, although the men still wore their swords. She nodded to the Ogilvys of Balnagrow, with whom she had had kind dealings even in the days of Clang-Causey, who resented them for his father's death; to Marjory Ochterlony brave and fine; to Blair of Balgillo and his wife; to the Grants of Freuchie and the long-lipped Menzieses of Glenogilvy, Cossins and Doonan: all now were friends or kin of the Lyons.

The Laird of Pitcur carried a great crimson hat into church. Young Huntly, of course, was not present, and if he had shown himself, swords would have been out. There was a feud between him and the Forbeses as there had once been between the Lyons and the Ogilvys, but not for so recent a cause: it was in fact forgotten why the two hated one another.

Yet, she must not think of hate today, when Elizabeth and her handsome young betrothed came hand in hand to the altar, knowing each other as well as if they had been brother and sister after all the years of upbringing together in Forbes' house. Jonet was pleased with young John Forbes. He had been in trouble over a duel with one of the Huntly clan some time ago, for he was quick though gentle. But there was no sign of the former trait as he smiled down at his bride. Frivolous Elizabeth looked beautiful, as always: her dress was of pale blue satin, and her head-dress fashioned of fresh primroses and their leaves. The pair made their vows, with the assembly watching. What reason could there be for any lack of fortune? They would surely live together long and happily, everyone thought. The bridesman, the Master's younger brother William, performed his duties quietly. There was one attendant for the bride, her sister Margaret. Jonet prayed that some among the company would take note of Margaret's youth and not of her sullen temper. She looked as well today as she ever could, but wore her flowers with disdain, as if they were too childish for her.

Afterwards there was feasting, and after that again dancing to fiddles on the green summer turf. Jonet had drawn aside among the watchers again feeling herself too old to dance. But a tall dark man came up to her whom she had seen in church. He was a Campbell, she knew already: a son of old Argyll. Campbells were either foxy or dark. She was aware of the steady regard of his grey eyes. She felt an unaccountable pleasure, and chided herself. Who was she, at her age, to take note of a young man?

"My lady Glamis, will ye dance with me?"

She shook her head, smiling. "I am an old woman. The mother of the bride should not dance." She would leave him with no illusions about her, already she was aware of that. Margaret sat nearby, the dreaded stubborn expression on her face. Jonet was about to direct young Campbell to her, when he said a thing which astonished her: its like had never been said to her before.

"Ye are of no age, and no time: and nor am I."

He must be fey: the Highlanders often were so.

She gave him her hand and he led her out, but she remembered the dancing less than the talk, and still more the silences.

"Ye are of the west," she said to him. "They are not as we

are."

Even his voice was soft and caressing, different from the brisk accents of east-coast folk. He smiled.

"It is a place of long sunsets and fair islands, and the arms of the lochs reaching to the sea. I would take ye there."

"Sir, I—" she faltered. She was used enough to discourage gallantry, but this was no philanderer. No one she knew had ever spoken like this man. Quite suddenly she allowed desire to rule her. It would be pleasant to have him by her. She thought of the lonely bed at Glamis, then briefly of Clang-Causey. This man would never bruise her as he had done.

She felt the colour flood her cheeks, and saw him smile, and felt the warm dry grasp of his hand.

"Ye are for me and I for you, Jonet Douglas," he said quietly.

They did not fall apart when the fiddles stopped and the bride and groom were bedded. His place was by her, she agreed: he would be always by her now, till the end.

"I am not rich," he had told her. "Skipnish is not so grand as one of your farms at Glamis. I was married young, and have one daughter there. My wife is dead. It was not as this will be, between the two of us."

He was simple and unpretentious. After they were married and living at Glamis she would remember their meeting, and how it was at once important to hide nothing from one another.

"I am a rebel, put to the horn," she had told him. "At any time the King may remember, and trouble both yourself and me."

"I will meet trouble and all else for your sake if I am let," he answered, the grey eyes steady. She knew she would be glad of his strong arm about her. Her feeling of being forever outside, a watcher, had gone. She was alive for the first time since she had left Tantallon long ago; young, fair and in love. In love at thirty! Others would laugh if they heard; then let them.

"What of your daughter?" she said once. But he disclaimed it. "She is cared for by her own kin," he told her. "She will never leave the west." So the thought of him as a father left her. It was evident that he was not close to his daughter, had perhaps never been close to his wife. Their two lives had spun together in the end like a random knotting of threads. She would do nothing against such a fate; how could she?

She had never, in all her years with Clang-Causey, known the full passion of physical power given and taken. If it had been only a day, or an hour, that they were together, she and Campbell, she would have bartered her share of heaven for it. As it was, by some mercy, they had almost two years; in the snow of winter, the green promise of spring, the colours of autumn above the burn. The world passed them by. There might have been no other place in the world but Glamis, and nobody in it but their two selves.

The children liked Campbell and did not resent him. Once he asked Jonet if she would like to travel with him, and bring them, to his own country. She thought for moments and then shook her head. "Some day, maybe," she said. It had come to her that Glamis was the place of her happiness with him, her loved and tended home of long years. Meantime, at least, she wanted no other; and the children would be strange in the west.

So the long lochs never saw Jonet Douglas, and the mountains reaching down to the sea.

22

When he was a child James V had been briefly betrothed to
King François' young daughter, Madame Madeleine de
France, but everyone knew by now that she was delicate,
said to be consumptive, and should never marry. In some
manner, therefore, James was betrothed to Marie de
Vendôme, whose father was a rich and powerful Bourbon.
The King was more particular than his own father had
been: he would not take a wife without seeing her first. He
set sail, but the luck of the Stewarts brought on a storm,
and Hamilton of Finnart, Lennox' murderer, strode to the
rudder and turned the ship back to Scotland. His
Majesty—he had made his title clear by now—was wroth,
and engaged on a second attempt lacking the presence of
Hamilton. It was important that this vessel should reach
her destination, for she carried, besides clothes and jewels,
a load of Scots gold, mined on Crawford Moor.

James had never before been abroad, not even as far as
England, where his mother would have taken him long
ago. Once landed at Dieppe in winter, he went mad a little,
going to Paris and seeing the shops, and buying himself a
great white plume of ostrich feathers for his hat, and a
great table diamond. Certain aristocrats looked down
their noses: it was not *comme il faut* for a king to run about
the booths like a market-woman. They were impressed,
nevertheless, with the handsome red-haired foreigner,
except that his French was halting.

Marie de Vendôme was impressed too, and fell lastingly
in love with the man who was to prove a fickle suitor. In
fact, her breath stank. James occupied himself all through
the betrothal feastings and shows with trying, somehow,
to win free of the situation. In the end he rode off,

promising to return.

He never did, and Marie de Vendôme demanded to enter a convent. By then, James had met with a gay cavalcade of courtiers, riding on a summer day. Among them was a girl in an invalid-carriage. They fell in love at sight, and as she was none other than the Princess Madeleine, to whom he had first been betrothed, the King of Scots announced that his later engagement was broken and that he wished to marry Madeleine de France and none other.

Even King François, that supreme cynic, told the truth: Madeleine indeed had consumption, would never endure the strains of marriage, of life in Scotland, or of childbirth. But love would take no denial: the young King of Scots surprised the King of France in his chamber where François had gone for a nap, they embraced one another and the promise was made. It was impossible that sixteen-year-old Madeleine should die: she was supremely happy.

They were married on a bitter January day at Notre-Dame, with the Crawford Moor gold set about in gilt cups at the guest-tables afterwards. Nobody had ever seen a pair so much in love. The Auld Alliance was pledged, remembered, approved by all.

The young couple spent all of the spring together in France, visiting here and there, but vastly content with one another's company in spite of James' bad French. But the time had come to go and they sailed on a good tide, with the little bride in furs to her chin and the hold weighed down with figured velvets and bolts of slashed silk. The Queen of Scots was said to be already pregnant. Everyone wished for a happy outcome. As for the Emperor Charles V, he had retreated from a planned invasion of France when he saw the Scots ships, mistaking them for a great enemy fleet. Nothing could have been more fortunate.

Young Huntly had been at the wedding in France, but, like many Scots lords, returned home before the King. He expressed his doubts about the royal bride to Jonet, sitting with Campbell in her warm hall.

"I doubt she will not live," he said. "It is too good to last. The weather here will finish her. The King jousts finely in France and has a high heart, but he knows not sorrow yet."

"Then he is content," said Jonet. Perhaps the moody boy would leave her her freedom now he had his much-loved bride to occupy him. No doubt Margaret Erskine at Lochleven would be wearing the willow: or had James forgotten her also? There was the boy Moray to remind him, and they said other bastards elsewhere. No doubt His Majesty had not thought of the future, only taking joy as it came.

"He should be content enough," growled Huntly.

"Vendôme gave him twenty thousand crowns, and the French King thirty thousand. All's blithe till that is spent."

"Do not grudge him his happiness," she said, and smiled at her husband.

The royal ship touched in at the north-east shore of England, driven there by winds. Several folk waded out to beg the King of Scots to come and be their ruler: they were fugitives from the Pilgrimage of Grace, to which Henry VIII had behaved with treachery and cruelty, executing many and hanging its leader, Robert Aske, in chains above York till he died. But although James spoke gently to them, he had enough ado with his own kingdom, from which he had by now been absent five months.

They came to Leith, and all the folk exclaimed at the joyous beauty of Queen Magdalen, as they called her. She was beloved from the instant she stepped on ground, by the people as much as by her husband. James seemed to have shed his gloomy fits, and was open with everyone, pleased that they should kiss his Queen's hand, which she gave them laughing, showing off her gold ring. Her colour was bright and seemed healthy.

They made their way to Holyrood, escorted all the way by shouting rejoicing people and the pealing of church bells. Not since the marriage of the Thistle and the Rose had such joy been in Scotland.

23

Huntly sipped his wine cautiously. Since the Douglas attainder he had made his peace with the King, and the Forbes marriage had offended him. Yet how could one be angered with fair Jonet Glamis, seated here by her fireside with her new husband? Campbell of Skipnish had been accepted by the neighbourhood since the time of last winter's snows, when he had come out with the men and dug for the succour of the poor cottagers, who had neither food nor fire and were overwhelmed to their chimneys' height by the weight of the frozen snow.

"Ye have seen the Queen?" asked Jonet. Huntly tried to describe the bright-cheeked girl, happy in her love, but he found it hard.

"I doubt she will not live," he said. "Her colour is not healthy. They say such folk breed swiftly. God grant that she may live to bear the heir, for lacking her the King will be sore at heart. Yet I doubt, I doubt."

"Surely, when she has sustained the voyage from France, she will mend?" asked Jonet. Campbell hung on her every word, watching her as if they had just met.

"I cannot say," answered Huntly.

There was the sound of a horseman without. It was Charteris, new come from Forfar. He entered with a grave face.

"Madam, there is ill news," her said. "They say the Queen is dead."

A chill went through the hall.

Magdalen had rallied, then fallen sick again at Balmerino, where she had been taken for the fresher air. The fragile girl had died only forty days after landing in Scotland and kissing the soil. It was said that the King kept very quiet nowadays, not even taking pleasure in his bastard son the Earl of Moray, of whom he was so fond.

"May God assoil her," said Jonet. "This harsh land was her death."

"It need not be the death of you and me," said Campbell. He came over to where she was and took her hand. "Ye are thinking of the King's mind, are ye not?" he said. "Whatever befalls I am with ye." And she took comfort from him.

At Holyrood, Queen Magdalen was laid to rest in the chapel, and the wine that was to have run in the streets at her coronation was put aside, and dead-bells rung. The mourners, candles and dismal chanting sounded where there was to have been such joy.

And the King, left alone, fingered his dead wife's figured and furred velvets, her cloth of gold, her narrow ruffs, her little jewel-coloured hats; and found no solace for his grief. He must fill his mind with other things. And he cast about, and remembered Jonet Douglas, Lady Glamis, who with her clan had long eluded him.

24

William Lyon was elsewhere, and it was some time before he heard of the marriage. When he heard, he let it prey on his mind for a while: then he galloped south, his horse's mouth foaming and the foam borne behind in white flecks on the wind. The tears on his cheeks were whipped salt into his mouth, and he was full of bitterness and anger. To have married another, a young man, a stranger; and kept him about her at Glamis! And she so chaste, never having admitted *him* to her bed in all these years of suing, and instead, now, at this moment, no doubt, they were coupling and murmuring together in the warmth of her chamber, rolling in lust upon the feathered mattress, kissing, slobbering against one another's flesh as they had done these many months . . .

Damn her! Fire burn her! Damn her for his long torment! To do her harm, to break the chain that bound him still, the only way, by death! Name her a poisoner! Condemn her, kill her! Take the man too! Take all she loved, but never himself! Very well, my Lady Glamis, ye have dreed your weird, and now, and now—the King . . . he could persuade the King of it all. James would believe what he wanted to believe, he had held his hand for years against this Douglas woman, on whom he could pin nothing slanderous. But now . . . two juries, refusing to appear . . . he himself, William Lyon, would be her jury and judge her, punish her; he and the King.

He reined in at the castle gate at last, and was shown to His Majesty where he was, idling with some jet and ivory device, sullen, sad, withdrawn. His face lightened when he saw William: they had become, in a way, comrades over the years.

William knelt. "Your Majesty will not credit the ill news I have to bear. That woman at Glamis would poison ye. She and her husband and her sons, her son-in-law Forbes . . . all of them are in the plot, and if ye were to rack them it would yield the truth from their tongues. I came at speed, as soon as I learned of it." It had been a good point about young Forbes. He had only just thought of it.

"Poison?" said the King. His fingers stopped playing with the device of ivory. "Lady Glamis wed again? Indeed? I did not know of that. There must be patience in such matters." He would find witnesses on this occasion, and have them bribed. The thought made him forget, for the time.

A slow triumph entered his mind. Such a charge would mean that he could bring the woman and her defenders, her accomplices, her husband, to Edinburgh in the end to try, and she would not be protected by her neighbours and kin, but by members he would choose himself, who feared him.

He gave a little, cold smile to William Lyon. Good William, who had long been loyal and who had had suspicions of the Glamis woman always, like himself! It would not be hard to convict Jonet Douglas, once he had hold of her person: the law said accusation was the root of the matter. That must be secured quickly, before she escaped with her new man.

He beckoned to a servant, and whispered something, and the man went out. James turned, still smiling, to William Lyon.

"I am grateful," he said. "Frequent my company."

And William lingered in Edinburgh, to hear what he might.

25

They had lain together in the great bed at Glamis, and thereafter fallen asleep in one another's arms. The summer night was short. Campbell awoke first, and after blinking against the light looked down at her, at her fair breast naked, the covers cast aside for heat, and her tumbled hair. If they had only had these past hours out of the whole of life, it would have been more than the sum and splendour of happiness. He knew it, gazing at her before she had wakened.

At the same time another sound, alien and yet half expected, came to him: the trampling of armed men. His mind's eye saw them come through the trees, across the green summer turf to the castle wall, and halt there. Then a shout, and the cry "The King's men!" The summer sun glinted on their armour. He could not yet see their faces.

It was true: they were here. He heard them. Had he known that this was to be their last hour together? He could foresee the future, the grey prison wall, perhaps the torture and the fire. He made himself turn to her and caress her breast and shoulder, her fair breast still naked to the day.

"Jonet, my wife, they have come."

She had hurried on her clothes in haste, hearing the trampling in the hall. Margaret rushed into the room still in her shift, her bedgown clutched about her, her face white with terror.

"Mother, Mother, will they never leave us in peace? Why are they come? They have taken my brothers, will they want me, too?"

"I will tell ye why they are here," said Jonet calmly. "It is because I am a Douglas. Hide yourself and they may not take ye, my daughter." But she knew well they would have taken everyone else, the two boys, perhaps others, and herself.

She went down, followed by Campbell in his tunic and hose, the full sleeves of his shirt rucked with haste. The hall was full of armed men, as it had been that time Gavin Hamilton came. But the men today wore the King's colours.

Their leader stepped forward. Behind him, she saw her two sons, already bound; the servants, and Charteris and John Lyon the old priest bound also, which angered her. Kate had followed.

"Ye are Lady Glamis?"

"I am." She heard her own voice light, as though the scene were not real, as though she had lived it before many times, and would do so many more. Yet in her heart she knew this was the last time.

"Ye are charged with conspiring in the destruction by poison of our lord the King's maist noble person: and of intercommuning with rebels."

She was amazed: he had recited the words as if he had learnt them by rote, and she had had no notion of such a charge.

"Poison?" she said. "I am innocent, and so are all my folk. Free the old priest, I beg of ye: he has done no harm."

"I am instructed to bring to justice in Edinburgh yourself, your husband Archibald Campbell, your sons, and your daughter's husband the Master of Forbes. The priest must come, for he may witness to your confessions. Make yourself ready to ride, Madam. We must go by full day."

Margaret will be safe, she felt her mind utter crazily. At that moment Margaret herself came running, the tears streaming down her face.

"Mother, Mother, I will have a care to Glamis till ye return. Have no fear for that. Mother, forgive me if I have not been obedient at times. I would the time were ours again, and you so good a mother."

Jonet kissed her daughter. What she was saying meant nothing except that it came from her heart. Margaret Lyon would be left at Glamis till she grew old alone. There would be no marriage for her; after this nobody would bind themselves to an attainted name, to their undoing. Jonet thanked God Elizabeth was safe. But as they rode by Kynedward her bridegroom young Forbes was brought to them, also bound, leaving Elizabeth alone and in tears.

"What is his fault?" she heard herself say clearly.

"Aiding and abetting yourself in your evil designs."

"Who has condemned him?"

"My lord of Huntly."

So the clan feud had simmered on. Jonet prayed for Elizabeth, the young wife left alone. What misfortune had come on them all! They had bound her own wrists and those of Skipnish, who protested angrily.

"Sir, my wife and I will ride to the King's order without ropes and cords, as though we were condemned criminals."

"Ye are so. She is named poisoner, and ye are art and part." And they tightened the bonds, lest he make his escape with Jonet. It was their farewell to Glamis, leaving the place rising pale and remote in the daylight. They would never again see the place where they had been happy. She remembered Clang-Causey and how he had not been so bad a husband. How enraged he would have been to be captured and bound! But maybe if he had lived, the King would not have dared act thus. There was no escape now in this world. Wherever I am, she thought, James Stewart will have me by the end. I should have foreseen it and not brought in those whom I love.

She reproached herself especially for Campbell's sake; for her two sons who were pale and crying; for young Forbes and Elizabeth: and for the innocent servants, who had been taken also, Charteris and Kate and John Lyon the priest, and the rest.

They did not reach Edinburgh that night, nor did they go by way of Innerpeffray. The Drummonds would have helped her there, and no doubt the soldiery had been told to avoid it. She saw its tower far off among the trees, in the gathering dusk.

They lay by night on horse-cloths in the summer grass, and the men took turns to watch while the prisoners slept. But Jonet did not sleep, nor did Campbell. Yesterday at this hour she had lain in his arms and had known quiet happiness. Tomorrow?

She sought him with her eyes. Least of them all would Campbell take kindly to prison. She prayed that his free spirit should not be broken. She sought him with her eyes, and the grey gaze met hers for, it might be, the last time. They would not let her be with him in prison. She could not bear to think that they might also torture his body.

Edinburgh Castle reared above them next day. They were taken in by the great gate, surrounded by guards. The two boys and Forbes were taken to one cell, Campbell to another, the servants and priest to a third. She saw them hustle Patrick Charteris away. It was as though she had lost a limb. She had not been able to speak with him, and it hardly seemed possible that the cruel rack would not wring lies from him like other men.

But she need not have troubled. Not one servant, let alone Charteris, said a single word to incriminate her: least of all Charteris, whom they racked till his joints sprang open. He kept silence except for screaming, and when words were demanded only would say that his lady was innocent, was innocent. Jonet prayed for them all, alone in her cell. She prayed also for strength for herself. The trial was tomorrow. So much haste, as if to prevent her from the very proof of innocence!

But she would outface them. All that night she spent in writing, without sleep, by a candle's light, then the dawn light, the speech which she would make, not only denying any attempt on the King but showing that it would have been impossible to have made it.

"Try to sleep, darling," she said to Kate, whom they had left with her.

26

Young John Glamis looked about the stinking cell in horror. He had never pictured himself in prison. He was a great lord, subject to none in all the land except the King. Ever since his father's death his mother had impressed upon him that he was a person of note, to give him confidence. As a result, John had swaggered, until yesterday when they had come and bound him with cords. Prison, and all its stench, and the summer sun picking out where flies rose, and stains on the floor and the walls! And he had had to perform his natural functions without privacy. The ridicule of it stayed with him, setting him on edge. But worse was to come. He knew it, even before they came, and they came soon.

They led him down to where the servants were. To see them racked might loosen his tongue, they hoped. John gazed at them almost without recognition. They were dirty and unshaven, even Charteris whom he had been brought up to regard almost as an oracle, the man who knew the answer to everything and never did wrong, the perfect servant. Charteris remained so, though the sweat stood out on his forehead now in great beads.

"My lady is guilty of the charge," they told him. "Give us the answer we need and ye are a free man."

"No! No! She is guilty of nothing."

Another turn. The screws creaked. "No . . ."

They racked the other servants. Not a single one incriminated John Glamis' mother. Towards the end he had been afraid they would torture him also, and surely if that agony came he would not be able to maintain the truth and would swear to anything, sign anything. The courage of the servants made him ashamed, and craven.

He felt wetness between his thighs.

They saw it. The torturer jerked his head and waited, ropes in hand. "My lord ... the like may be done to yourself, if ye will not sign."

Sign what? Afterwards he could not remember anything but the scraping of the quill. He could not have told anyone what he signed, except that it seemed to please them, and after that he was left in peace.

George, his younger brother, shivered against the wall. Elizabeth's husband young Forbes was with them, and had not witnessed the torture or been threatened with it, so he was still proud and angry.

"It was Huntly did it," he said. "I saw his man riding on the road. His clan have aye hated us. There is naught to concern your mother. It is between myself, and Huntly. When I meet with him he will know my sword."

They stared at him. By now they knew the charge against Jonet Glamis: intending to poison the King, causing the death of her first husband by poison, and intercommuning with rebels. The last they knew was true. But why had they all been caught in the net?

It was Huntly, young Forbes maintained, and believed it till the day they hacked off his head on Castle Hill, nearby the pyre which was to burn Jonet, his mother-in-law.

27

They had led her into the Exchequer courtroom. This time the jury were there in strength, their unknown faces turned towards her avidly. They were mostly taken from the south-west, and her name meant little to them. The indictment was read amid a hush. This was different from the usual horse-thieving, stabbing, sudden murder, theft, arson they were used to. This woman must be from Satan, she seemed so fair. They prepared themselves to pass judgment. But first the victim must speak. Jonet had prepared her own defence, and stood throughout, reading aloud in a clear voice that could be heard by every man there. The King was not present.

"Those that hate my brother Angus are enraged, because he is not in their power, that he might fall a sacrifice to their malice. And they now discharge their spite upon me, because of my near relation to him. And to gratify their revenge with my blood, they accuse me of crimes which, were they true, deserve the severest death. But, since it is the prerogative only of God to punish men or women for the faults of others, which belongs to no judge on earth, who are obliged to punish everyone according to their personal crimes, you ought not to punish in me the actions of my brother, how blameable soever."

The jury stirred. She was clever, this woman. But the graver crime had not yet been dealt with. They waited. The clear eyes ranged over them, then returned to the paper she held.

"Above all, ye ought to consider if those things I am accused of have the least appearance of truth. For what gives the greatest evidence either of the guilt or innocence of an impeached person is their former life. What fault could any hitherto lay to my charge? Did any ever reproach me with anything that is scandalous? Examine into my former conversation. For vice hath its degrees as well as virtue, nor none can attain to a perfection in either, except by long practice." She looked at them again, whether virtuous and vicious. Certainly she dissembled well.

"If ye can find nothing reprovable in my conduct, how can ye believe that I am arrived all of a sudden to contrive this murder, which is the very height and perfection of impiety? I protest I would not deliberately injure the most despicable wretch alive." A memory came to her of William Lyon, and his years of whining at her.

"Could I," she said loudly, "then make the murder of my sovereign, whom I always reverenced, and who never did me wrong, the first essay of my wickedness? None are capable of such damnable and unnatural actions, except such as are in desperate circumstances, or such as are hurried into plots by reward or revenge. My birth, and conditon of life, puts me beyond the suspicions of the first of this kind; and for the latter, since I was never injured by the King, how can I be suspected to thirst for revenge?" A forward lad, his hand on her breast in dancing long ago . . .

"I am here accused of purposing to kill the King. And to make my pretended crime appear more frightful, it is given out that the way was to be by poison. With what strange impudence can any accuse me of such wickedness who never saw any poison, nor know I anything about the preparation of it? Let them tell where I bought it, or who procured it for me?"

The jury nodded together. This was a point. The matter seemed to have been undertaken in great haste.

The clear voice went on. Campbell, who was present and bound, never took his gaze from her. He knew that it might be the last time he would see her on earth. All his love was in his looking. Their time had been so short, but had encompassed the whole of life. Had they had many years together they could not have known greater love. He was content, except for the injustice.

"Or though I had it," Jonet said of the poison, "how could I use it, since I never came near the King's person, table, nor palace?"

Robert, Lord Maxwell, leant over to Lord Somerville. They should go to the King, he murmured. There could be no proof of guilt, except Lord Glamis' document. The two conferred with the rest and slipped out shortly. Jonet went on with her defence, her eyes resting for an instant on Campbell of Skipnish where he sat.

"It is well known that since my last marriage with this unfortunate gentleman, I have lived in the country, at a great distance from the Court. What opportunity could I have to poison the King?"

She felt strength come to her. She was almost smiling.

"Ye may see by those circumstances which give light on such matters that I am entirely innocent of those crimes I am charged with. It is the office of you judges to protect injured innocence. But if the malice and power of my enemies be such—" She thought again of William, for she had known of his going "—be such, that whether guilty or innocent I must needs be condemned, I shall die cheerfully, having the testimony of a good conscience. And assure yourselves you shall find it more easy to take away my life than to blast my reputation, or to fix any real blot upon my memory." Were not those the words priest John had used to her? She felt a clear lightness come. She thought of him, and of her sons in prison, and of Forbes and Campbell and the servants, who had done no wrong.

"This is my last desire of you, that I may be the sole object of your severity, and that those other innocent persons may not share in my misfortunes. Seeing my chief crime is that I am descended of the family of Douglas—" her smile grew "—there is no reason that they should be involved in my ruin. For my husband, son and cousin—"

she spoke thus of Forbes "—are neither of them of that name or family. I shall end my life with more comfort if ye absolve them. For the more of us that suffer by your unjust sentence the greater will be your guilt, and the more terrible your condemnation, when ye shall be tried at the great day by Almighty God, who is the impartial judge of all flesh."

The two lords were admitted to the presence of the King. By his side was an ordinary-looking man, dressed in rowan-tanny. The lords made their views known.

"Sire, the witness has proved the articles of impeachment, and according to the law of the land deserves death. But all of us are agreed that she cannot be guilty, despite her son's writ."

"She has beguiled you," said James.

The man beside him nodded.

"She is subtle," remarked William Lyon. "It were pity to spoil the law because ye are all of ye men. She is well known as an enchantress. I myself was under her spell for many years, but now see the day clear." He lowered his pale eyes. They could not like him. But the King turned his head.

"Sire," they said, "it is a case of *summa justitia summa injuria*. We are concerned at the thought of injustice." Their minds were beginning to waver: had they indeed been beguiled? She was most fair.

"It is surely," said Somerville, "best to observe equity and mercy such as that for which Your Grace is known."

The King frowned: the older title was less preferable to him than Majesty.

"It is easier," went on the lord, "to absolve a criminal than to condemn an innocent person."

"Give it time," said Lord Maxwell. "The witnesses should be examined, and their honesty tested."

"Ay, they may have been bribed."

The King flushed: the remark was an accusation of his

own honesty. He felt his stubbornness grow. He turned to William Lyon again.

"What think ye? Ye are acquaint with her life and manners, and the circumstances." He knew he need not specify further. William was like himself, and could give good reasons.

William spoke. At the back of his mind was fear: if time were given, his own lying might well be uncovered. He answered the King.

"Everyone knows Your Majesty's clemency, for ye are by nature merciful. Ye have entrusted these judges with the exercise of the royal dignity. It is their office to preserve the innocent and punish the guilty. There is no doubt in my mind that this woman deserves punishment: remember her lord's death, how swift it was."

That was the day after I danced with her, thought James. The remembrance made him feel foolish. And what a fool he would look if the woman were set free! She was a Douglas. He had sworn vengeance on them all. The Tudor glance regarded the two jurors, standing with eyes fixed on the ground. They were increasingly unsure of themselves.

"I order you to proceed according to justice and the laws of the land. There is a book called *Regium Majestatem*. It contains all ye need to determine this case. Abide by it, and trouble me no more. There is nothing to prevent your doing your duty like men of justice and honour."

"Then she must burn?" asked Lord Maxwell, who knew the book.

"She must burn, and do it at once: this affair has gone on long enough. She has troubled the peace for years."

They went back to the Exchequer presently, and conferred with the rest. The King was set on my lady's death. It would be harmful to themselves did they not defer to him. In the minds of every man was this King's difference from his father: he could be spiteful.

They gave the sentence of death. Jonet stood to receive

it.

"When is it to be carried out?" she asked them.

"Today."

"Give me time to prepare my soul. What of the rest?" She seemed calm, and not in terror of the sentence.

"The old priest may go. The rest must remain, and my lord the Master of Forbes must die, as your accomplice. The King has mercifully granted that he may be executed, not hanged."

Campbell is safe awhile, she thought. He had risen and was straining at his bonds.

"Ye cannot do this thing! It is against all justice! Let me go to my wife!"

They did not prevent her going to him, and they kissed.

"It is farewell for a time," she said. "Have no fear: I am not afraid."

As she went out, the jury bowed their heads, stricken.

She had asked for a priest, and they brought old John Lyon to her, hands hanging swollen and limp from the torture. She took his hand in both of hers, raised it, and made the sign of the cross.

"They have judged me," she said, "and I would have my soul assoiled before I die."

"Have you any guilt, my daughter?"

"None, I swear it before God. I would only confess such things as are in my mind; resentment, perhaps; lack of forgiveness for moments. I feel now that I may forgive them all, and go to my death and meet God."

"Almighty God will greet you, have no fear. They may touch your body as they have touched mine, but our souls they cannot reach, and beyond this life, and its faults, ye are freed and blessed. Say a little penance, a Pater and Ave and Gloria: and go without fear. Think of the martyrs: their agony was fierce, but soon over, and how blessed they are now!"

"You yourself have suffered. I feel anger at them for

having put the rack on you, an innocent man and old."

"I have offered my suffering to God. Do you the same, and recall sweet Christ on the cross, where He hung three hours. Your agony will not be as long, and you have not been scourged, mocked, and crowned with thorns, nor carried your cross all the way."

"I do well to remember Him. He bore the sins of all the world: I bear only my own."

"Go in peace, my daughter." He absolved and blessed her, then there was the taste of God on her tongue. After he had gone she went to the window and looked out on the clear summer day, and the town's reek below the Castle, and the great loch with its chapel, far off. She had an unreal acceptance that this was the last time she would look upon it. But the fire would be real enough. She prayed that she might not flinch, or cause their mockery because she seemed afraid. She was not so: courage came to her from some source. Where she was going, at any rate, there would be justice, and love.

28

She came out of the grey prison to the sudden brightness of the July day. A crowd was waiting, their faces turned towards her. As she walked to the stake they swayed, and there was some shouting. She realised that they would have rescued her, but the King's guards turned them back. The sun shone on their armour. They were placed at intervals along the front of the crowd.

The stake was waiting, with tied bundles of faggots at its foot. Beyond it was the block where Forbes would die. She saw him as they led him out, and made the sign of the cross. He did not attract such attention as herself. Wryly, she acknowledged the fact that many had come to see her die.

There was one in the crowd, besides William Lyon, whom she saw skulking. This man was of the middle height, and wore a plain tunic and cap to hide his hair. But she knew him, as he her: it was the Gudeman of Ballengeich, come to witness the burning. Jonet did not curtsy: he would not want to be known. He is trying to forget his young wife's death, Jonet thought, and had time to feel sympathy for James. For herself, she was not afraid. In all ways she had lived her life, and now must go. But the manner of it! She prayed for courage, that she might not tarnish her Douglas name.

A man was tying her hands to the stake. She knew that even he was a sympathiser.

"Lady, have no fear, the smoke will get ye afore the fire," he murmured. She was tied now, motionless at the stake. She saw them come forward to light the faggots, which took readily in the summer heat. To make it doubly sure, they flung on torches, their flares pale against the brightness of the day. It might all have been a masque, happening to someone else. She did not yet feel pain. She spared time to think of Campbell, helpless in prison. *This land need neither be your death nor mine.* Were those the words he had spoken? It was near enough. How did her son fare, and his brother? They had told her Glamis had signed a confession and that had aroused pity in her, for he must have been tortured, or seen torture. He was not strong in mind or body, and neither was his brother. How did it happen that she had borne two weak sons?

The crowd were still murmuring. Word had gone round that the condemned woman was innocent, and they loved her beauty. The King stood erect, his hard glance focused on her face. If I quail in any manner, she thought, he will be pleased. She resolved not to give him this final satisfaction, but could feel the heat creeping, creeping, while the flames broke out here and there among the sticks. A pall of smoke had risen. Presently it reached her, and after a first effort she no longer tried to draw breath. She must let it stifle her before the burning. Blood-red darkness came to her, and she was no longer able to breathe and could not move to find the air. Then she knew no more.

Archibald Campbell of Skipnish heard none of the sounds from the Castle Hill. Later they came and told him his wife was dead, having suffered with great bravery. He knew bitter anger. Jonet's dear body to be scarred by flame, her spirit separate from him even for hours! Had her sons been told? Yes, they had been told. The Master of Forbes had suffered also, on the block.

That night Campbell resolved to escape, to trust no more to the mercy of such a King. He had given money to the gaoler. The man brought him a rope, knowing it was safe now that the foremost prisoners were dead. It was dark by then, and very late at night. Skipnish writhed through the narrow way and sensed the Castle rock yawn below him.

But he could not judge exactly in the dark. He clung to the great height, said a prayer, slung the rope to a jutting piece of rock, and let himself down. The rope did not reach the ground, but surely it could not be far off. He let himself slide and then go, and fell, and fell.

In the morning they found a group of huddled limbs on the grass below. Campbell was dead, his spirit already gone to Jonet.

There was little to tell of the rest. John Glamis bought his way out of prison on the death of James V, and made a good marriage. The old priest John went back to Glamis, and died in obscurity. Charteris was heard of there no more: he would not serve the boy who had betrayed his mother. Young George Lyon died as a result of his imprisonment.

William Lyon had sidled into the crowd to watch. There was a strange trembling in his limbs. He saw Jonet come out, heard the crowd's pity and felt it sway and jostle, and saw the King's guard close in. He clenched his fists against his tunic to steady himself. They had bound her. They were lighting the faggots now, and throwing torches on the flames. A pall of smoke hid her from him. When it died down, she was nothing more than a blackened twisted thing, a dead thing, no longer desirable . . .

He fainted, kept on his feet by the close-pressed crowd. Presently he came to himself, his mind black and empty. Then into it came remorse, like a flood. He could no longer endure to look at the thing bound to the stake, smell the burning flesh and hair. He turned and elbowed his way out of the crowd, and when he had got to the edge of it he vomited, a thin stream of yellow bile dripping to the cobbles, ruining his clothes. He wiped his mouth with his hand, and staggered off. They were executing young Forbes now, and the blood would run scarlet. Someone said the King had granted leave, out of mercy, that the young lord should not be hanged, drawn and quartered. The executioner held up the bleeding head by its hair.

"So die all the King's enemies."

The words rang out into a sudden silence. There was nothing to be done any more; the day's show was over. The headless body was covered with a cloth. They said he had been a fine young man, newly married.

A figure in grey came up to William. It was the King, in his disguise.

"Ye are ill, my friend," said James, and gave a steadying arm. The secret eyes betrayed no feeling. William felt his guilt overwhelm him and he fell to his knees. He heard his own voice gabbling, she had been innocent, innocent. He had lusted after her and when she would not oblige him, had devised her death.

The King frowned. The man's kneeling made his own presence known, and though the crowd dared show no hostility, there were looks in his direction, as though they did not love him. He bent his mind to listen to William and was horrified. Was the man mad, to tell him such a tale? Within himself he knew that, whether there had been truth or lies, he had destroyed Jonet Douglas because of her name and because she had rejected him.

He drew away from the kneeling man and spoke coldly.

"Ye had best get yourself overseas: I want no more of ye."

William was weeping. He saw the King stride off, and was left in an empty space while the crowds streamed past. Soon he would be alone with them, with the headless corpse and the blackened ashes that had been Jonet Glamis.

He scrambled to his feet and ran, away from the scene, away from the ruin that he had helped to bring about, towards Forth water, that would take him away from such a place . . .

He made his way to Flanders, lived for a time, then died in misery.

After the burning the Glamis servants had been set free, Kate among them. She saw the rest come, red-eyed, limping, but with their heads high. They had not betrayed their lady, though her own son had; that was known already. Kate looked for Charteris, and saw him in unbelief; he had turned into an old man, uncertain where or how to place one foot before another; even his height was shrunken. She went to him.

"Lean on me," she said. "They didna rack me."

He looked at her, as though she had been any stranger; then did as she asked and leant his weight on her a little. They moved slowly down the hill with the rest.

Presently she spoke. "Would ye gae back to Glamis?" He was silent for a moment and she saw his mouth's bitter curve.

"Never," he said. "I wouldna serve *him*."

"Then shall we gae south, to my lord's lands?"

"My lord of Angus is under attainder. None will dare shelter us in the south." He spoke wearily, as though it had been the way for long; as indeed it had. She thought of old Kilspindie to whom none had dared to give a drink of water that time at Stirling. "To England, then?" she said. She had quietly assumed that they would go there together. To be with him, even though he might never be her lover, was all she asked now of life.

"We need writs for England." Slowly, his wits were reawakening; the horror was behind them; somehow, they must live on.

"Surely if we say we are my lady's servants, the Border folk will let us pass. We cannot ask the King for writs; he would maybe take heed that we are free, and cast us into prison again." She was not to know, for no one yet knew, of the confession of William Lyon and that, surely, His Grace would accordingly be merciful.

"Wherever ye say. It matters little."

"I have money," she told him. They could maybe hire a place in a vegetable-cart for a while, and then see what could be done once they were beyond the city wall. She began to look about her as they came to the level of the street; carts would be coming at day's end from the Grassmarket. Presently they found a carter and she went up to him.

"Do ye gae south? My husband is ill." She did not care if Patrick heard; if she was to shelter and succour him, she must call him her husband. The carter looked at her ill-favoured face and nodded.

"I can take ye to Penicuik."

"That will do."

They climbed in, Patrick painfully, and the cart rumbled off towards the south gate. In the end they would reach England and my lord, and as the King there was favourable to him they might stay. But they would continue together whatever befell, thought Kate; she had made her man accustomed to her presence. She would be there, by him, always. The cart travelled on through the fading day.

29

Angus had heard the news. He sat, red-eyed, with their brother George in a tavern near Hampton Court outside London. George's young son James, an unpleasant secretive boy, was with them, his sly glance fixed on the door.

Angus was silent, gazing into the depths of his tankard. In it he saw Jonet's fair face, tried not to picture the flames scarring it, twisting it, reducing it to ashes. She would die bravely, like any Douglas. But a curse on the man that had destroyed her! Had he ever had an affection for that boy? It was burnt, gone with Jonet on the lifting of the four winds. Kings were the same everywhere: this one here, who still professed to be his friend, had cut off the head of his own wife last year—if Anne Bullen had indeed been his wife. She had left him a girl with red hair and spider-thin fingers, named Elizabeth after the King's mother. Now again Henry hoped for an heir. Oneself was the only one pilloried, because of that bitch in the north. They said Queen Margaret had dropsy. Hopefully she would die soon, and then he would marry again and get heirs, with all pardon to Madge, who assumed that she would be Countess of Angus in due course. He was fond of Madge, but a son would be better, without royal blood to tarnish and destroy his life. Poor Madge had newly won out of the Tower where she had been put by reason of her Howard lover. Both were too near the throne of England. Madge would never be like other folk: she was too proud. God knew whom she could marry.

"Ye are silent," grunted George. Angus did not reply and George looked away. He knew the reason for the silence well enough. Rue the day when his brother had married a queen! He, George Douglas, had had no time for her, nor for her brother, though it was not safe to say so even in an inn, so near the palace King Henry had filched from Cardinal Wolsey at the time of the fall from power. James V was a Papist, like his mother. He had no conscience; these folk took it all to the priest and thought that God absolved them. He, George Douglas, knew better. A man might learn of his own salvation from reading the Bible. It was not to be spoken of aloud yet, but the day would come. If he ever won back to Scotland, he would live as he chose, and speak as he chose, and James his son the same. And they would not forget what the royal Stewart had done to their sister Jonet Glamis. Such a crime could never be forgotten.

"More wine?" said Angus, still as though he were far away.

"Ay."

The wine was brought, and the three sat drinking in silence. It was the only safe condition in England, unless one were within one's own four walls. Maybe the day would come when a man could speak out: here, and in Scotland.

The King had heard William's revelation with horror, then later asked himself if he had not, from the beginning, known the man to be false. He had desired vengeance on all the Douglases and had obtained it, that was all. Yet he began to find his solitary hours intolerable, no longer even taking pleasure in disguising himself as the Gudeman of Ballengeich. He tried to write verse. Some was good, the rest bad. He flung away his quill, and set out, on St Andrew's Night, for Glamis, which was now his property. The ride north through November mists was eerie: it was as though the ghost of Jonet haunted him, and yet he could not feel her near him, any more than she had been that far-off time at Stirling when he had tried to make love to her, without the achievement.

The fairytale towers rose out of the mist at last, and he was fascinated. He would take pleasure in visiting Glamis again and again, even after his second marriage to a tall, nobly descended Frenchwoman, Marie de Guise. King François had adopted her as a Daughter of France. She bore James V two sons, but both died, and the birth of a third child, a daughter, was of no interest to the King: by then he had sent his friend Oliver Sinclair to command the Scots army against an invasion from England, and there had been a resounding defeat at Solway Moss, almost as tragic a day as Flodden. The King wandered for a few days and then died, they said of a broken heart, at Falkland. He took his own memories with him; the time he had tried to make love to an Egyptian woman in the forests, and her kin had come and beaten him and forced him to carry a great load of wood on his back: and the time he had hanged the Border rebel, Johnnie Armstrong, after promising him pardon. His uncle, Henry VIII, had long been his enemy: perhaps it dated from the time of the persecution of Angus, and destruction of his sister Lady Glamis. In succeeding centuries it was mistakenly stated that Jonet had been burnt as a witch.

Glamis remains, with its memories. It is one of the fairest castles in Scotland.